Orphan Journey Home

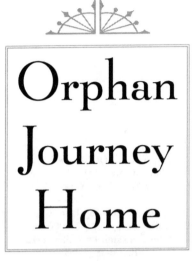

Orphan Journey Home

LIZA KETCHUM

illustrated by

C. B. MORDAN

AN AVON CAMELOT BOOK

AVON BOOKS, INC.
1350 Avenue of the Americas
New York, New York 10019

Copyright © 2000 by Liza Ketchum
Interior illustrations copyright © 2000 by C. B. Mordan
Interior design by Kellan Peck
ISBN: 0-380-97811-3

Library of Congress Cataloging in Publication Data:

Ketchum, Liza, 1946–
    Orphan journey home / by Liza Ketchum ; illustrated by C.B. Mordan
    p. cm.
    Summary: In 1828, while traveling from Illinois to Kentucky, twelve-year-old Jesse and her two brothers and sister lose their parents to the milk sickness and must try to finish the dangerous journey by themselves.
    [1. Frontier and pioneer life—Fiction. 2. Voyages and travels—Fiction. 3. Orphans—Fiction] I. Title. II. Mordan, C. B., ill.
PZ7.K488 Or 2000   99-042649
[Fic]21—dc21

First Avon Camelot Printing: March 2000

Printed in the U.S.A.

OPM   10 9 8 7 6 5 4 3

www.avonbooks.com

For the children who have followed this story in newspapers across the country—may all your journeys lead you safely home.

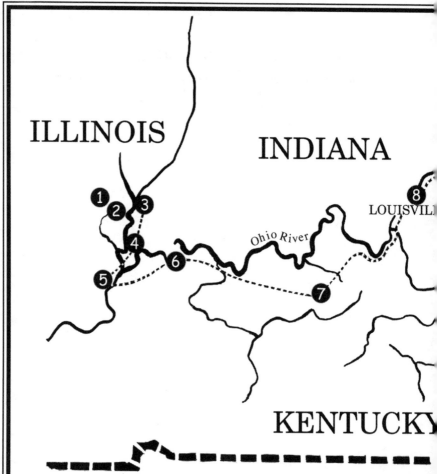

ILLINOIS

INDIANA

LOUISVIL

Ohio River

8

KENTUCKY

TENNESSE

Map Key

1. West bank of the Little Wabash River
2. Little Wabash crossing
3. Wabash River crossing to New Harmonie, Indiana
4. Posey County, Indiana
5. Shawneetown, Illinois
6. Henderson, Kentucky
7. Near Hardensburg, Kentucky

CINCINNATI

OHIO

LEXINGTON

Acknowledgments

It has been both a thrill and an honor to write a story for the newspapers and to learn how many readers, young and old, take great pleasure in following a story from one week to the next. My deepest thanks to Avi and his wife, Linda Wright, who launched me on this wonderful journey and offered the story to newspapers across the country through their innovative company, Breakfast Serials. Thanks to my editor, Ruth Katcher, and my agent, Gail Hochman, who have been faithful shepherds to the story since the beginning, as well as to Justyn Moulds, who graced this book with her careful eye and sharp attention to language.

I feel very lucky that C. B. Mordan was chosen to

illustrate both the newspaper serial and this book. His wonderful scratchboard drawings captured the family and the time period exactly as I had imagined them in my own mind.

I am most grateful to the dedicated staff members of Newspapers in Education, a national program that has brought this story, and others like it, to millions of readers across the country. In a number of cities, dedicated teachers and/or staff members also created innovative study guides to accompany the story. I am especially indebted to NIE staff and teachers connected with the *Boston Herald;* the *Dayton Daily News;* the *Desert News;* the *Essex County News;* the *Hartford Courant;* the *Hampshire Gazette;* the *New Bedford Standard-Times;* the *Lewiston Sun Journal;* and the *Lexington Herald-Leader* for their enthusiasm and commitment to children and education.

Many readers, historians, and librarians helped me research this story. I received invaluable assistance from staff at the American Antiquarian Society in Worcester, Massachusetts, the Boston Atheneum Library, and the University of Kentucky Press. A number of careful readers in Kentucky gave me information about old maps and routes. I send grateful thanks to Millard Allen, whose historical map answered many of my questions about early trails. Thanks also to Timothy Strawn, of the Ohio Masonic Home, who shared his knowledge of Freemasonry with me and a group of interested teachers.

I am most grateful to the following friends, family members, and colleagues, who helped with historical and medical questions, offered support, or gave critical readings of the manuscript at various stages:

Chuck Bogni, Eileen Christelow, Janet Coleman, Ann Dillon, David Giansiracusa, Susan Goodman, Karen Hesse, Lisa Jahn-Clough, Bill Loman, Bob MacLean, Sarah Stone, Katherine Turner, Katherine and Bryan Wilkins, and Janet Zade. I salute my parents, Barbara and Richard Ketchum, who offered expertise on questions ranging from antique rifles to veterinary disease, and my sons, Derek and Ethan Murrow, who are always there when I need them.

Finally, my deepest thanks to my husband, John Straus, who has championed this story from its inception, read every version with care, and pushed me onward when the journey seemed as difficult for me as for the Damron children, struggling to find their way home.

Orphan Journey Home

1

Papa's News

June 15, 1828.

West Bank of the Little Wabash River, Illinois.

"Jesse! Moses!" Mama calls from the cabin. "Finish your chores and come quick. Papa has a surprise."

Mama sounds excited. I look up from milking Nettie. "Moses, did you hear?"

"I'm not deaf." A forkful of hay tumbles from the loft and lands near Nettie's feed box. The cow flicks her tail against my face.

"Whoa, Nettie." I crook my elbow hard against her leg to keep her still. What could the surprise be?

My brother's black boot swings out over my head. His bare foot shows through the worn-out sole. "You have a hole in your boot," I say.

"You have a hole in your *head,* the way you snuggle up to that cow." Moses clunks down the ladder.

3

"I'm glad milking is *girl's* work." He says *girl* as if he were chewing one of Mama's pickled turnips.

"Wonder what Papa wants to tell us?" I ask.

Moses scowls at me, then forks hay into the feed boxes. "Nothing good," he says. A mosquito whines near my ear. I aim a stream of milk at the bug, but miss.

"Don't waste good milk," Moses says, and stomps out of the barn.

I sigh. Moses and Papa have been acting strange lately. Yesterday morning, Papa dropped his hoe in the cornfield, went off in the wagon, and didn't get home until after dinner. And Moses keeps riding away on Ginger, his mare. He carries our rifle, but he comes back with no game, and won't tell me where he's been.

"Jesse!" Solomon rushes into the barn, out of breath. "Mama says hurry. But don't spill the milk." He plugs his mouth with his thumb, his big brown eyes waiting on me.

"I'm coming." I follow Solomon to the cabin, lugging the heavy bucket. It's hard not to slop milk on my skirt. What is Papa's surprise? Did he sell Nettie's calf in Shawneetown? Maybe he bought us some pretty calico from a riverboat trader. Maybe Mama will help me sew a new dress that doesn't bind my chest and pinch under my arms.

I stop, feeling the warm mud seep over my toes. What if Papa bought me new shoes? But I don't dare dream about that. My feet have been red and raw all spring, ever since my old boots wore out. Mama promised to stitch me some moccasins, but we haven't

4

had any soft deerskin in a long time. Papa won't hunt deer while they're raising up their new fawns.

When I come inside, there are no packages on the table. The pale boards are scrubbed clean. Mama sits at one end. Solomon scrambles into her wide lap and sits very still. Louisa perches on her stool, clutching her doll. Its dried apple face is as pale and puckered as her own. Papa's beard is wet and his hair is brushed back as if it was Sunday.

I feel funny. Why is everyone so quiet? I glance around the cabin to see if I've missed something, but it seems the same. Soup bubbles in the big iron kettle over the fire. Mama's herbs are dusty, hanging from the rafters, and the little pool of sun near the open door makes the rest of the room seem gloomy.

"Set the milk down, Jesse," Papa says. "Moses, come sit with the family."

My older brother shakes his head. He's leaning against the wall, his arms folded over his chest. His eyes are as dark as Papa's, but they don't have Papa's warm shine. "I know what you're going to say."

I'm surprised at my brother's rudeness, but Papa ignores Moses. He turns to me as I scoot in next to Louisa.

"Jesse," Papa says. "I have good news. Can you guess?"

I twist toward him on my stool. "You went to Shawneetown and bought me some shoes?"

Papa looks ashamed. "No, Jesse. I wish I could. I know your feet are sore. But this might please you even more. It's something you've wanted for a long time."

What could I want more than shoes? I glance at

Mama. Her smile lights her round face like a harvest moon. My heart trips in my chest. "We're going home?" I whisper.

Papa nods. "Home to Kentucky?" I screech. "And Grandma?" I jump up, knocking over my stool, and dance a little jig, my bare feet thumping the dirt floor, then grab Mama and squeeze her so tight I knock Solomon off her lap.

"Hey!" my brother whines, dusting himself off.

"Jesse Damron! Calm yourself." But Mama's not really scolding me. She folds me into her soft arms and hugs me back.

"When?" I ask.

"Soon as the mud dries," Papa says.

"Then you'll be here the rest of the summer," Moses says. He stands in the doorway. He's grown so tall, he has to duck his head to fit under the frame. "The trail from here to the Wabash is axle deep in mud, thanks to all this rain."

Mama eases me to the side and peers up at Moses. "Son, what's eating you?" she asks.

Moses ignores her. He glares at Papa. "You promised," he says. "You said if our family moved again, we'd head west, where the prairie goes on forever."

We hold our breath. "I know," Papa says. "I'm sorry." He looks down at his hands.

"Then you'll have to travel without me," Moses says. He yanks on the latchstring. The door closes behind him and the room turns as dark as his scowl.

"William, stop him," Mama begs.

Papa goes to Mama and puts his arm around her shoulders. "Those rumors he's hearing about the prairie are flying around like crows. But they're only tall tales. Just like the ones that drew us here. Remember?" Mama nods, and Papa pushes back wisps of her yellow hair so he can look down into her eyes. "We heard the soil was black as ink, without a stone in sight. That I could earn more money farming than I ever could building with stone." Papa shakes his head. "No one warned us about settling on bottomland, near the river. And how could I know the corn crop would be so poor this year?"

Solomon wraps his arms around Papa's leg. "Why did Moses go away?" he whispers.

Papa smiles down at him. "Don't worry. He's just feeling his oats, like our frisky calf in the barn. He'll come with us in the end."

I wonder. Ginger whinnies, and I hurry to open the door. I see Moses swing onto the mare's bare back.

"Moses!" I cry. "Wait up!"

But Moses doesn't even turn his head. He grabs the reins, kicks his heels against Ginger's belly, and canters off toward the forest. In an instant, my brother is gone.

2

Grandfather's Kentucky Rifle

June 15, 1828.

West Bank of the Little Wabash River, Illinois.

I lie awake a long time after dark, waiting for the *clop-clop* of Ginger's hooves, but the only sound is the far-off rush of the river.

Even though I try not to fall asleep, I dream about men fighting and wake up hot and sweaty. I hear voices outside. I sit up slowly, trying not to jostle Louisa. How can a skinny six-year-old take up so much room? The corn husks rustle in our pallet as I peer out the tiny square window.

Moses is back. He stands close to the house with Papa. The moon slips in and out of the clouds, so I can barely see their faces. Moses's legs are planted wide, like sturdy oak trees. "So you plan to sell the sheep and the calf? How are you fixing to farm?" Moses asks Papa in a low voice.

"I'll go back to working with stone. Every town needs a mason. Or I'll open a grist mill. They say times are better in Kentucky now."

Moses steps closer to Papa, until he's right below my window. "I know you think this wet bottomland gives the girls their fevers," he says. "But there's better farming on high ground. We don't need to go far."

I hold my breath. Are we moving because of Louisa and *me*, and the terrible sickness Mama calls "fever and ague"? We were sick off and on all last summer.

"Moses, I'm not a farmer," Papa says. "I learned that the hard way. And you've seen the young corn— only half our seed sprouted. What will we eat in the fall?" His voice breaks. "Look at the little ones, son. They're pale and scrawny as fledglings. Besides, your mama misses her family. And she wants you children to have an education. It will be a long time before we see schools out here." He sets a hand on my brother's shoulder. "Come on to bed. We have a lot to do in the morning."

Moses turns away. I strain to hear his voice. "I talked to Mr. Flower, at the English Prairie settlement. He says the western prairie is bigger than the sea. Maybe I'll try my luck there." He waves his hand toward the west and leans that way, as if he can see that open prairie land from here.

I hold on tight to the window ledge. So my brother ran off to English Prairie tonight. Maybe that's where he went those other times, too. Why didn't he tell me? I hate secrets.

Papa's voice is so soft I have to hold my breath to

hear him. "Suit yourself," Papa says. "But you're likely to get bound out, traveling alone."

Bound out. Those words make me shiver. Mama has told us stories about orphan children who get snatched up like stray chickens. She says people treat bound-out children like slaves, and they can't get away until they're grown.

"I'm almost fourteen," Moses is saying, drawing himself up.

Papa laughs gently. "You've grown tall, son, but you still have a child's face and voice."

Moses ducks his head. I feel sorry for him. Papa shouldn't have said that.

"I'm sorry, Moses." Papa's shoulders are slumped. "How do you think I feel? I don't want to go back to a slave state. That's one of the reasons we chose Illinois—they don't allow slavery here. Owning someone else is wrong—the idea turns my stomach. But your Mama and I are too tired to start over in a new place. We've worked ourselves to the bone, building this cabin, clearing the timber, trying to grow corn where it's too wet."

A cloud scuds across the moon, hiding their faces. "I can't stop you if you want to go west," Papa says, "but you'll have to travel on foot. We need your horse for the trip. And as for your mama—don't expect me to make excuses for you. You'd better talk with her yourself."

I've never heard Papa give such a long speech. As he heads for the door, I wiggle back under the feather bed, breathing slow, as if I'm asleep. Papa climbs the ladder into the loft. I hear Mama's soft voice, then Papa's, but I can't make out the words.

This time, I pinch myself to stay awake, waiting to see what my brother will do. Papa starts to snore and Moses slips inside, leaving the door open. Moonlight washes over the table, where Mama's johnnycake sits waiting for breakfast. I watch through half-closed eyes. Moses rummages in Mama's rag bag, pulls out a clean scrap of calico, and wraps up the cornbread. He bundles his clothes, then tiptoes to the pallet he shares with Solomon and leans over him, touching his head.

My heart is beating so fast I'm afraid my brother will hear it. Moses stands beside the open door a second, then reaches up over the frame. Grandfather's Kentucky rifle hangs there. I grit my teeth to keep from shouting, *You can't take our rifle! How will we eat, if Papa can't hunt?*

Moses shoves the leather sack of gunpowder into his pocket, tucks the rifle under his arm, and leaves without making a sound. I pull on my clothes, my fingers shaking as I button my dress. When I slip out the door after him, the clearing is empty. Sadie, the mule, snuffles at me from inside the fence. The river hisses along below the willows. Which way did he go?

Moses must be headed to English Prairie. If Moses is gone, our family will topple, like Mama's chair when its leg broke.

I pick up my skirts and run barefoot along the muddy track that leads north from our clearing. An owl hoots above me, or maybe it's a bear. Sometimes we hear wolves in the forest. What if a wolf finds me before I find Moses? If I get lost in the woods, what will happen to me?

﷼ **3** ﷼

A Scream in the Forest

June 15, 1828.

On the trail to English Prairie, Illinois.

Not far from the cabin, I hear a strange sound, like a puppy whimpering. I stop running, my breath coming ragged in my throat. Then I inch forward and hide behind a tall tree. Moses is sitting on a fallen log, his head in his hands—crying!

"Moses!"

He jumps to his feet, grabbing the gun, then slumps back down when he sees it's me. He swipes at his tears, and I pretend I don't see them. "You shouldn't be here alone," he warns me.

"I came to find you." I point to the gun. The silver stock gleams in the moonlight. "You can't steal Grandfather's Kentucky rifle, the one he used in the war against the British. Papa will never forgive you

17

if you take it away. Besides, we'll starve without our gun!"

"I know." He balances the gun on his knees. "I can't leave, but I don't want to go back to Kentucky, either. Don't you see?" He looks up at me. "That's the old life, Jesse. The new life is out west, where there are so many buffalo you could walk across their backs for miles. There's a river called the Mississippi that flows all the way to the ocean. And miles of black soil with no stones or stumps to clear away." He grabs my hand. "Papa's forgotten those steep Kentucky hills and the hollers where the sun only shines at noon. Come with me, Jess. We'll have an adventure."

Even though I don't want Moses to go on alone, I can't imagine leaving my family. Besides, I remember Papa's warning. "I'm afraid of being bound out," I say. "I'm only twelve. And what about Grandma? What will she say, if we don't come home together?" I think about how Grandma cried when we pulled away from her cabin two years ago, how she ran after us on her short legs, waving until we couldn't see her anymore.

"We don't even know if Grandma is alive," Moses says in a tight voice. "We haven't had a letter in six months."

"Don't talk about her that way!" Now he's scaring me. "You have to come with us," I tell him. "We can't get on the Shawneetown ferry without you. Sadie won't obey anyone but you."

He hesitates, and I think maybe he'll change his mind, but then he waves me away. "There are plenty of men at the ferry crossing. They'll push that stubborn mule onto the boat." He hands me the rifle. It's so heavy, I can barely lift it. "Take this home. I'll travel without it."

"How will you eat, if you can't hunt?"

Before he can answer, we hear a scream, more horrible than the time Mama found a rattler in the cabin. The hair prickles on the back of my neck and my hands are so clammy I nearly drop the gun. "Someone's killing Mama!" I shove the rifle into my brother's hands. "Come on!"

"Jesse, wait!" He grabs my elbow. "That's not Mama. It's a panther."

A panther? My legs tremble, like the time I had the ague. Papa told me about panthers, but I've never seen one. As big and fast as a wolf, he said. Even worse, they can climb trees. "It's near the cabin," I cry. "We've got to bring the gun back. Hurry!"

We run toward the clearing. Clouds hide the moon. We stumble and trip in the dark. Papa shouts our names and the panther screams again. It sounds as if it's above us, in the trees, in the shadows beside the trail, in front of us, then behind. Moses grabs my hand and pulls me along. I scramble to keep up with his long strides.

I hear another scream, but it's not the panther, it's the mule. My heart jumps and stutters against my chemise. "It's after Sadie," I whimper.

We come out of the woods into the clearing. "Papa, we're over here," Moses calls out, low and frightened. Shadowy moonlight lands on Papa, who stands in the doorway, gripping an ax. Mama holds up the lantern beside him. Louisa and Solomon peer out from behind her nightdress. When Papa sees us, he warns, "Stay back!"

19

We freeze at the edge of the woods. The panther perches on the fence while Sadie circles the pasture. It's the biggest animal I've ever seen; bigger than Papa. The panther's long tail twitches like a cat about to pounce. But this isn't a cat, and it's not after a mouse. It wants our mule. I bite my lip to keep myself quiet.

Moses rams a ball and gunpowder into the barrel of the rifle and raises the gun to his shoulder. I stick my fingers in my ears. "Don't shoot!" Papa yells. "You'll kill Sadie."

Too late. The panther shrieks, Moses pulls the trigger, and the gun kicks back, nearly knocking him down. I grab him from behind, my ears ringing.

We wait, shaking, for the smoke to clear.

4

What's Wrong with Mama?

June 16–19, 1828.

West Bank of the Little Wabash River, Illinois.

Moses is lucky: his shot misses Sadie. The panther disappears and Mama pulls us into the cabin. We fall asleep, huddled on her pallet, while Moses and Papa stand watch outside.

In the morning, Louisa and I find Papa and Moses leaning against the barn, dozing in the sun. Papa's hat is pulled down over his eyes. He startles awake when he hears us and stands up, setting the rifle aside. "Morning, girls," he says. "We had us a noisy night, didn't we?"

Moses groans and rubs his neck. I glance at him, then at Papa, waiting for him to scold us for running off. But he seems proud of Moses. He shows us the trail of blood the panther left behind, spattered across the straw in the barnyard. "Your brother wounded that big cat pretty bad," he says. "We'll have to keep the animals shut in until we sell them. No one wants to meet up with a panther who's wounded and ornery. I've never seen one that big—must have been ten or eleven feet from his nose to the tip of his tail."

Louisa's skinny hand slips into mine. "Will it come back in the daytime?" she asks.

Papa shakes his head. "Not likely. But you stay close to home, just in case. Help your mama pack up. I hope we can leave soon. This sunshine will dry the mud."

He picks up his hat, dusts some straw off the brim, and heads for the cabin. Louisa plucks at Moses's shirttail. She asks the same question that's buzzing around in my head. "Are you coming with us?" she says.

Moses scowls. " 'Course I am," he says. "Come on, let's get some breakfast." He walks off without looking at me. Louisa skips to keep up with his long steps.

I stand there, watching them go. Why did Moses change his mind? Must be that panther spooked him. Or maybe I said the right things, after all. I smile to myself. Now we're headed for Kentucky—and the Little Sandy River—together.

We spend the next three days getting ready. Papa carts the calf and Mama's sheep off to English Prairie to sell. The calf bawls as Papa ties him to the back of the wagon. Nettie bellows in the shed. I close the shuttered window over Nettie's stall and try to rub the knob between her ears, but she tosses her head, trying to get loose. Her legs are trembling. "Hush,

Nettie," I say. "You can have another calf next year. Papa needs the money for our ferry rides."

Mama calls me into the cabin. "Can you climb on the table and hand me down my herbs?" she asks. "Reaching up there makes me dizzy today."

I scramble onto the table and dance a little jig on the smooth boards, rattling our metal cups. "Settle down, Jesse," Mama says, but she's laughing. I untie the bundles from the rafters and give them to her one by one. The herbs are dusty. I sneeze, nearly dropping the next bunch. "That's burdock," Mama says. "Good for poison ivy." She packs it away in her herb box, and tells me something about boneset, but I'm not really paying attention. A worried feeling prickles in my belly, as if I ate too many wild onions.

"Will that other family move out of our old cabin, when we get home to Kentucky?" I ask.

Mama looks surprised. "Of course not, Jess." She places the last bunch of herbs gently in the box and snaps the lid shut. "They bought it from us when we left. Besides, the soil was too thin up on the ridge. We'll be better off near the river, 'specially if your papa wants to start a grist mill."

My cheeks feel hot. "I thought we'd go back to our old house. Where will we live?"

"With Grandma, until we get settled."

I close my eyes, trying to see Grandma's cabin in my mind. I remember her narrow porch, and her little bedroom at the back. If I close my eyes, I can almost hear the Little Sandy River lapping at the sandbar where Louisa and I used to play—but I can't remember anything else. "Is there enough room?" I ask.

"We'll double up, like we always do," Mama says.

"Anyway, it will still be warm when we get home. Some of you can sleep on the porch."

I'm not sure I like that idea. I think about our old house, perched on the brow of a steep hill. When I sat on the front step, I could see all the way down the misty valley. I had my own pallet to sleep on, tucked away behind the chimney. No Louisa to dig her sharp elbows into my back at night and wake me up with nightmares.

But still, I'm glad we're leaving this cabin. It seems dark and dingy now, with our clothes in bundles by the door and Mama's herbs packed away. "Who will live here, after we're gone?" I ask.

"A family from Indiana is moving in." Mama sinks into her chair. "Your papa didn't have the heart to tell them how hard it is to make a go of it here. I hope they won't blame us if they fall on bad times." She rubs her arms. "My goodness, Jesse. Isn't it chilly today?"

"No, ma'am." I give her a funny look. The sun is so hot, Papa let the fire go out after breakfast. Even my feet are warm. But Mama is shivering, so I find her soft wool shawl, the one she knit this past winter, and drape it over her shoulders. "Take my spinning wheel outside, won't you?" Mama asks. "We'll have to fit it in the wagon somehow." She leans her head back and closes her eyes. "Even my bones feel heavy," she says. "I'll just rest a minute."

Mama's wheel is almost as tall as I am, so I call Louisa to help me carry it across the dirt floor and out the door. Louisa's arms are so thin, she can hardly hold up her end. We set it near the wagon. Louisa disappears inside and comes back with her stool. She holds it up to Papa. He's sitting on the wagon seat, braiding a new whip from willow strips. Solomon watches from the wagon bed. "Can you put it in the wagon?" Louisa asks. "I'm not big enough."

Papa shakes his head. "Leave that here," he says. "We don't have room."

Louisa's face crumples. "But Mama is bringing her spinning wheel."

"Of course. She needs it, to spin her wool into yarn," Papa says. "I'll make you a new stool in Kentucky. All our furniture stays, for the next family."

Louisa starts to whimper. "But it's *my* stool," she says.

"That's enough," Papa says. His eyes are dark. Solomon peers over the wagon at us, his thumb in his mouth.

"Don't make Papa angry." I smooth Louisa's stringy hair and pull her toward the cabin. I know how she feels. It hurts to think of some other family eating johnnycake at our table. "Let's pack your dolls," I tell her. "They'll be sad if we leave them behind."

We go into the cabin. Mama is asleep in her chair with her quilt pulled up to her chest. Her face is pink and her mouth is wide open. A tin cup half full of milk sits on the table. Her tongue is coated white, like she dipped it in whitewash.

"Why is Mama sleeping now?" Louisa asks in a soft voice.

"I don't know." It feels funny, having Mama asleep in the daytime. I don't dare wake her up. Louisa and I whisper as we pack her dolls inside her clothes bundle.

We spend all afternoon loading the wagon. Solomon and Louisa get fussy, so Papa lets them make a cozy bed in the back of the wagon. They play house with Louisa's dolls while we pack our things all around them.

After everything is snug inside, Papa hitches Sadie between the traces. "Let's back the wagon into the barn," Papa says, "in case it rains tonight." But Sadie balks, bracing her feet like trees. Her ears flatten against her head and her top lip crinkles up, showing her yellow teeth. Papa leans against her shoulder, then flicks the new whip near her head, but she won't budge. Finally, Moses takes her bridle, clucks to her, and talks slow and quiet. She takes one careful step back, then another.

"See?" I tell Moses, when she's in the barn. "Sadie only listens to you."

"Don't be foolish," Moses says. But Papa winks at me. I feel warm inside—but only until we go back to the cabin. There are no smells of supper cooking, and Mama is still sitting where I left her.

"Shh. Mama's sleeping," Solomon whispers. We gather around her chair and Papa shakes her shoulder. "Rebecca," he says. "What's wrong?"

Her blue eyes open, round and surprised. "Why, look at me," she says, "falling asleep when there's so much to do! I guess I'm all done in from the packing." She heaves herself up out of her chair and looks outside. "Goodness—the light's going. How long have I been asleep?"

No one answers, and Mama says, "Good thing I planned a cold supper tonight."

Nettie bawls from the barn. Papa gives me a

sharp look. "She'll be full up, with the calf gone," he says. "Better get on with the milking."

I nod and fetch the bucket, dragging my feet. I can't keep my eyes off Mama. Doesn't anyone else notice? As she lifts the knife to cut the cold johnny-cake into squares, her hands shake like dried leaves in the wind.

✙ 5 ✙

Burning with Fever

June 20, 1828.

Crossing to Posey County, Indiana.

Papa wakes me before sunup the next morning and sends me out to milk Nettie. She smells funny and she won't stand still for me at all. Maybe she knows we're leaving. She stamps her feet and knocks over the bucket. Milk splashes my skirt and runs into the straw. I come back with an empty pail, but Papa tells me not to worry. "We can't carry it with us anyway," he says.

We're all too excited to eat. Mama is quiet, but she seems better. Papa helps her climb up into the wagon with Solomon and Louisa. As Moses cinches Ginger's saddle, Papa beckons to me. "Sadie's pulling a heavy load," he says. "You and I will walk up front. We'll keep Sadie moving."

I'm glad. I don't want to ride in that jouncing wagon. Moses swings up onto Ginger and I lag behind just a minute. I take one last look around our little farm. It seems quiet and lonesome. No smoke trailing from the chimney. No more sheep tugging at the silky grass. The barn door creaks in the wind.

Sadie leans forward into the traces and the wagon rumbles slowly down the track toward the Little Wabash. "Hurry up, Jesse!" Solomon calls. I run to catch up with Papa, my bare feet sliding in the mud. We're off to Kentucky!

We ford the Little Wabash in a shallow place, then cross the Wabash itself on our first ferry ride. Just as I thought, Moses is the only one who can coax Sadie onto the boat. He holds out a handful of dried corn and she trots forward, the wagon rumbling onto the ramp behind her. The ferrymen pole us across to a town called New Harmonie, on the Indiana side of the river. "Folks here started a brand new community," Papa tells Mama as we leave the ferry. "The women have the same rights as the men. Imagine that!"

Moses snorts. "We'd better not stay long," he says. "It will just give Jesse big ideas."

I toss pine cones at his hat. He kicks up Ginger and trots on ahead of us.

New Harmonie is new and grand. I stare at everything. The town has a big brick church, taller than any building I ever saw, two sawmills, and lots of brick houses. As we come around a corner, the door of a small log cabin bursts open and children come running out. A tall girl, a little older than Moses, stands in the doorway watching them. She's holding a book. I stop and point. "Mama!" I cry. "Is that a school?"

Mama nods. "I guess so, Jesse." Her voice is weak. "Come on now." I walk beside the wagon, dragging my feet. For a minute, I wish we could live here, but Papa snaps his whip over Sadie's head and the wagon jerks forward. We roll on through town and follow the river south.

Two days later, we're traveling through country Papa calls The Barrens. Scrubby trees not much taller than I am line the trail. The wagon sinks up to its hubs in the ruts, just as Moses predicted. Nettie hates plodding through the deep mud, so I have to walk behind the wagon to keep her moving. I flick a stick at the cow's rump. Her legs tremble whenever we stop. I guess she's as tired as I am, slopping along this wet track. Mud cakes the hem of my skirt and squishes through my bare toes.

I glance at Louisa, playing with her dolls in the back of the wagon, then at Solomon and Moses. They're riding Ginger together. I wait for them to catch up to me. Solomon's legs stick out almost straight on either side of the mare. His chubby hands clutch her mane. He grins down at me. "I'm taller than you are," he sings. I grab hold of Ginger's bridle. She jerks her head, and Solomon nearly slips off.

"Hey!" Moses wraps his arm around Solomon's waist. "Let go." He kicks up Ginger and they leave me standing in the mud.

I slip and slide past the wagon to catch up with Papa. "Why can't I ride Ginger?" I ask him.

"She's too skittish," Papa says.

"It's not fair. No one else has to walk. Can I trade with Louisa for a while? She has shoes."

"She's too small to keep up," Papa says. "I'm walking, too, Jess. I guess that means you and I are the strongest." He rumples my hair. "Go on, see to Nettie. We don't want her to wander off."

I stand aside while the wagon rolls past me. I don't feel strong. My legs are tired and my belly is empty. How will I ever make it to Grandma's, if I have to walk the whole way?

We follow the Wabash River until dusk, when we make camp. I tether Nettie to a skinny tree to milk her. She lowers her head to the ground, breathing hard. "Easy, girl," I say. I stroke her flank but she kicks at the bucket, just like last night. Dirt spatters across the foamy milk. I pick out as much dirt as I can before I carry the bucket to the wagon. Luckily, Papa doesn't see. Everyone but me drinks a big creamy cup at supper.

Later, Mama has a chill again, so Papa covers her with extra quilts in the wagon box. Louisa climbs up on the wheel and peers down at Mama's face. "Do you have fever and ague, Mama?" she asks.

"I don't think so," Mama says in a soft voice. "I'll be better in the morning. You all stay dry under the wagon."

Louisa curls up next to Solomon and me. She wiggles and whimpers like a kitten. "Be still," I tell her.

Louisa puts her mouth to my ear. "Mama's tongue is brown," she whispers.

I open my eyes wide, trying to see her face, but it's too dark. "Don't make up stories," I say.

"I'm not. It *is* brown. I saw it." She turns away, pulling the blanket off me. I yank it back, too tired to fight. I don't want Papa to scold us. An owl hoots from across the river, and the ground is hard. Worries about Mama keep me awake for a long time.

I wake up shivering and scratchy with mosquito bites. The morning fog makes everything clammy. As I snuggle close to Solomon, trying to get warm, I hear Papa call Mama's name. "Rebecca," he says. "Rebecca, speak to me." Papa's voice is hoarse. He doesn't sound like himself. I scramble out.

"Papa, what's the matter?"

"She's burning with fever," Papa says. I stand on tiptoe and peer into the wagon. Mama's round face looks mottled, like a dapple gray mare. "Run to the river for water," Papa orders.

The Wabash is so muddy and swift, I almost lose the bucket. Papa sponges Mama's forehead, then her wrists. Mama moans. Louisa was right: Mama's tongue is brown as dirt. My heart beats fast. I crawl to the back of the wagon and pull out Mama's medicine box. Why didn't I listen, when we were packing up her herbs? I stare at the twiggy bundles, trying to remember what Mama taught me, all those times we went into the woods or out on the prairie to gather plants. "She made me chew on willow bark, when I had the ague," I say, clambering back to Papa. "Shall I fetch some from the river?"

He shakes his head. "I think this is the milk sickness."

Milk sickness? Mama never told me about that

disease. I don't know what to give her. My hands are as clammy as the fog crawling over us. "Is she going to die?"

"I pray not." Papa stares into Mama's face as if he's never seen it before.

A prickly feeling gnaws at my belly. I think about the dirty milk we had last night. Maybe that made her sick. "How did she get this milk sickness?" I manage to ask.

"From the cow, I guess." Papa strokes Mama's face. I can't look at them. Everyone but me drank the milk. What if they all get sick? I jump down, run to Nettie, and throw my arms around her neck. My hand brushes her nose, and I freeze. Instead of being soft and moist, her pink nostrils are hot as embers. Her sides heave in and out and her head hangs down low. "Nettie's sick, too," I cry.

"Jesse!" Papa shouts. "Stay away from that cow."

I hurry back to the wagon and bury my head on Mama's soft chest. She mumbles something. "Mama," I whisper, "it's me, Jesse." She doesn't answer, and Papa tugs my sleeve. "Go find your brother."

Moses is fishing downstream. When I bring him back, Mama is worse. Solomon and Louisa wail at her feet like the world is ending.

I guess it is.

⚜ 6 ⚜

My Blood Runs Cold

June 24, 1828.

Posey County, Indiana.

Mama lingers one more day and night before she closes her eyes and leaves us forever. We forget to eat, and no one sleeps after she's gone. Nettie dies, too. I want to scratch the cow one last time behind her ears, but Papa won't let me near her.

After Papa covers Mama with their wedding quilt, I edge next to him and whisper the secret that's gnawing at my belly. "Nettie put her foot in the milk, the night Mama got sick," I tell him.

Papa pulls me close. His face is ashen above his beard. "The sickness was inside Nettie," he says. "It didn't come from her dirty feet."

I'm still scared. Everyone else drank the milk. Will they die, too?

"Where will we bury Mama?" Louisa asks in a quivery voice.

"On high ground," Papa says. "She hates the damp river bottoms." He glances at Moses. "We need to build a coffin." He clears his throat. "Be sure to explain that your mama is heavy—the box needs to be short and wide." He gives Moses some money. Moses drives the wagon back upstream to a sawmill for some pine boards while we search for Mama's last resting place.

Papa holds our hands and we climb a bluff high above the river. The sunshine melts the wisps of fog, wind ripples through the prairie grass, and a white oak spreads its leafy branches in a wide circle. Papa's voice breaks as he looks around. "She wanted to live in a spot like this," he says. "If only I'd listened."

My own heart is too full of cracks to comfort Papa. When Moses comes back, I take Solomon and Louisa to pick dandelions and other wildflowers while they build the box. Papa and Moses set the coffin in the wagon and lay Mama gently inside. We cover her with her soft gray shawl. Sadie strains, drawing the wagon to the top of the bluff. Did Mama grow heavier from the weight of our grieving?

Papa calls us over to say good-bye to Mama. Louisa clutches Mama's hand. She's crying too hard to speak, and Papa draws her into his lap. Solomon says, "Night, Mama," as if she's only going off to sleep. Moses kneels to whisper in Mama's ear, then stumbles away, his hands over his face. He hasn't spoken to Papa since Mama died. I guess he's thinking that if Papa hadn't made us leave, Mama would still be alive.

I tell Mama I love her. "I'll learn about your medicines," I say. "I promise." But who will teach me, now she's gone? I kiss her forehead.

When Papa nails the lid on the coffin, Solomon screams. I take Louisa and Solomon away and hold them tight while Papa and Moses dig the grave. It takes a long time. They lower Mama gently into the ground, and we scatter daisies and dandelions over the pine box. Papa brings me the leather Bible. "Read your mother's favorite psalm," he says. "And those verses about the mansions."

The book feels like a stone in my hands. I read, *"The Lord is my Shepherd."* Mama loved that one because of her sheep. And then I find the verses Papa wanted. *"In my father's house are many mansions. . . ."*

Mansions? I puzzle over that one as I read. I try to picture Mama in a tall, brick house, like slave owners have in Kentucky, but I know Mama would never live in a place like that. She always said she loved our cozy cabin. Now she's cramped in a tight box, forever.

I close the Bible and give it back to Papa. I think of Mama's gentle smile, her wide, soft lap where I loved to snuggle when I was small. I can't watch Papa fill in the grave. I run away and fling myself down in the tall grass, sobbing until I fall asleep, and wake up feeling gentle pats on my back. "Jesse," Louisa whispers in my ear, "Papa wants you."

Papa sits on the ground, leaning against the oak tree next to the mound of earth. He sends the others away and beckons me close. His face is as gray as the fog drifting in over the Wabash. He holds out Mama's leather diary, her pen, and a bottle of ink.

His hands tremble. "I want you to write a letter for me in case I'm not with you long." As he speaks, I notice his tongue. It's all coated with white—the way Mama's was when she first got sick. My blood runs so cold, I think maybe winter has come in May.

"No," I whisper.

"Jesse, I may have the milk sickness, too. You must be prepared." He grips my hand. I struggle hard not to cry. How can we live without Mama *and* Papa?

"Papa, if we're orphans—will we be bound out?"

"Not if I can help it. But since I can't write, you need to take down some words for me. It's a blessing your mother taught you to form your letters. Listen well. It's up to you now."

⚜ 7 ⚜

Tecumseh's Ghost

June 24–26, 1828.

Posey County, Indiana.

I try to form my letters carefully, but my hand
shakes. Papa stares across the prairie while he
speaks, as if he's already left us.

"My fellow Masons," he says. He waits while I
write, then goes on. "My children travel home to their
grandmother, on the Little Sandy River. Please give
them safe passage. They are not to be bound out. I
ask for your help and protection. . . ." I'm not sure
how to spell that big word. I want to run to Mama
and ask her, and then I remember: She can't teach
me anymore. So I write it all the best I can, including
his oath at the end, that these are his words, "written
in my daughter's hand."

Papa explains that there are Masons in many

towns. "They take care of widows and orphans. They'll keep you safe."

He holds the letter, squints at it, and shakes his head. "No matter how hard I try, the letters wiggle around like tadpoles," he says. "Your mama was always after me to learn. Now it's too late." Tears stream down his cheeks. He takes my hand. "You teach the little ones," he says. "And keep studying as best you can. Your mama wanted that for you. She was always cross with me for taking Moses out to work with me, when he should have been learning. She hoped you'd all go to school in Kentucky."

"We will if we can, Papa. I promise." I bite my lip, trying not to cry, while Papa signs his name with awkward letters. He calls to Moses, "Bring a candle and the flint."

Moses lights the candle and lets the wax drip onto the letter. Papa dips his heavy signet ring into the melted wax and presses hard, leaving his initials, W. J. D.—William Jesse Damron—next to his signature.

"Now the Bible, Jesse," he says.

I do as Papa asks, although I wish he would rest. Drops of sweat stand out on his forehead. He lays his hand on the leather cover and swears that he has written the truth, folds the letter, and hands it to me. "Keep hold of this," he tells me.

Moses steps between us. "Give it to me. She'll lose it."

Papa shakes his head. "Not if she puts it in her bodice. No decent man or woman will take it from her there."

I'm not sure who has the redder face: Moses or

me. I turn away and slip the letter under my chemise. It feels bulky and awkward against my skin.

"Now," Papa says, "listen hard, both of you." He explains the route home. "Take a riverboat to Shawneetown. This trail is too muddy, following the Wabash. I don't want you getting stuck. Then you'll cross the Ohio into Kentucky." He tells us the towns to head for. I get confused. They all sound the same. "Henderson, Hardensburg," he says. "Then Shelbyville, Frankfort. Lexington. Paris. To Blue Lick on the Licking River—"

"Wait!" I say. "You're going too fast." He repeats the towns, and this time I write them down on the back page of the Bible. Then Papa and Moses draw a map. Papa tells us the names of the roads, the mountain passes, even the trees and taverns. "After the salt lick," he says, "there's a buffalo trace to Tygart's River. Follow that trace, then turn right, toward Old Town and the Little Sandy."

"What's a buffalo trace?" I ask.

"It's a trail carved out by herds of buffalo. They always know the best route from one river valley to the next. You follow their footsteps, you can't go wrong."

Papa's voice is getting weak. I'm sorry to make him talk more. "How will we find Grandma's house?" I ask.

"You'll pass the sawmill," he says. "Then it's a few miles to the big white oak. It's the second turning, not the first—"

"I know the way from there," Moses says, interrupting. My brother's fists are clenched, as if he might punch somebody. Papa closes the Bible and makes us repeat the route back to him three times, just the way Mama helped me learn my letters.

"Good," Papa says at last. He holds out the Bible. "Place your right hands on the Holy Book." Moses and I do as Papa says, our hands touching on the leather cover.

Papa looks up at us. His eyes are red and wild-looking, like a colt that's never been broken. "Swear you'll bring Solomon and Louisa home to your grandma," Papa says.

"I swear," I whisper.

Papa waits for Moses. "Son?"

Moses's voice breaks. "I swear, Papa. But how?"

To my surprise, Papa takes Moses in his arms as if he were a little boy. "You'll find a way. You're strong children."

When Moses stops crying, Papa asks us to help him pull off his boots. We unlace them and wiggle them off one at a time. Papa reaches into the toe of his right boot and takes out a wad of bills. "I've kept all our money in here," he says. "You'd best wear my boots now, Moses—I know yours are too small. The boots make a good hiding place. Guard them with your life."

Papa's voice is even thinner now. He points to our gun, standing against the tree. "Keep hold of your grandfather's rifle. If you need money, sell the stock. Your grandfather used to say it was worth two hundred dollars."

Two hundred dollars! I stare at the gun. I can't imagine anything costing so much. Papa twists the signet ring off his finger and hands it to me. "This is yours now, Jesse. It also belonged to your grandfather, Jesse Damron. He was as tough as you are. That's why I gave you his name."

The ring is too big for any of my fingers, so Papa ties it around my neck on a cord, his hands trembling. The warmth of Papa's fever lingers against my skin.

Later, I study the list of herbs and medicines in Mama's diary. I make a tea for Papa from dried boneset leaves. Mama wrote that they bring out a fever.

"Can I help?" Louisa begs. We gather mullein, which sprouts on the prairie, and wrap the fuzzy leaves around his neck, like flannel. We make a soft bed for Papa in the wagon and take turns sponging his forehead, but nothing helps. Just like Mama, his tongue turns brown, his hands and feet are cold as ice, and his voice gets all choked up when he tries to speak to us.

In two days, we've lost Papa, too.

Moses can't build a coffin alone, so we wrap Papa in the wedding quilt. Papa is heavy and tall. Moses and I stagger, carrying him over to the oak tree where we buried Mama. How can we dig such a big hole?

We start the grave at dusk, when the little ones have cried themselves to sleep. Moses breaks up the sod with an ax and I shovel out the dirt behind him. Soon, my hands are raw and blistered. I'm cold as ice inside. Neither one of us cries or says a word.

Suddenly, we hear rustling in the grass. "Who's there?" Moses calls.

No one answers. Moses grabs the ax and we edge close together. A stocky man strides toward us, his cheeks and eyelids painted scarlet. His long, crow-black hair brushes a hatchet dangling from his belt.

51

His moccasins are attached to leather leggings that reach up to his thighs.

"A Shawnee," Moses whispers. "Don't move."

As if I could. My feet feel stuck to the prairie. Could he be the ghost of Tecumseh, the great Shawnee chief? They say no one ever found his body after he was killed. Papa told me that once, before I was born, a great earthquake made the Mississippi River run backward. The Shawnee people believed Tecumseh was so mad about dying, he stomped his foot and made the earth shake. They say his spirit still haunts the forest.

My teeth chatter as the Shawnee glares at us with fierce eyes, then folds the quilt back from Papa's face. He tamps Mama's grave with his moccasin and reaches his hand out to me.

What does he want? I can't even swallow. I drop the shovel and hold out Papa's ring. "Jess, don't," Moses groans. "We might need it, to get home." But I don't care. Anything to keep us safe.

8

Orphans

June 27–28, 1828.

On the banks of the Big Wabash River.

The Shawnee doesn't want the ring. He picks up the shovel and helps us bury Papa. Maybe the red paint made him seem so fierce. I'm ashamed of my fear.

I cook johnnycake while Moses and the Shawnee work together. Moses uses Nettie's bucket to scoop out the dirt as the Shawnee loosens the soil. When their knees disappear into the hole, I turn my back. It's too sad to watch.

After the grave is filled in, I wake Solomon and Louisa. Moses and I carry the little ones to the twin mounds of dirt. Solomon is heavy in my arms, but I can't let him go. Moses holds Louisa tight, too, as if she were a baby. Moses and I say a few prayers over Papa, and the Shawnee sings a long, lonesome song

55

that makes us cry. Moses lays cut willow branches over the graves to keep the wolves away while I feed the Shawnee some johnnycake. He gives us two dead quail from his leather pouch before he disappears. Next morning, there are no tracks from his moccasins in the tall grass. No trace of him at all.

When I wake up, I ache everywhere from all the digging, but nothing is as sore as my heart. We're *orphans,* I think. The word sounds lonesome in my head. To feel closer to Mama, I read her diary again. "Stewed dandelion greens make a healthy tonic," she wrote. I remember the dandelions, blooming out in the open, that we picked for Mama's grave. I collect the bitter greens and cook them while Moses loads the wagon. Solomon puckers his mouth and spits them out. "Ugh," he says.

"You can't make us eat them," Louisa says, pouting. "You're not Mama."

To my surprise, Moses gobbles his down and says to the little ones, "You have to mind your sister and me if you want to get home safe."

Solomon and Louisa scowl, but they swallow their greens just the same. I give Moses a secret wink to thank him.

Before we leave, we mark the graves with a scrap of pine board, writing Mama and Papa's names with a charred stick from the fire. Moses divides up Papa's money. "Some in each boot," he says, "and the rest in my shirt pocket." He shoves his feet into Papa's sturdy boots and hands me his old ones. "Try them," he says. But they flop around on my feet, even with socks on. I wrap my feet in flannel, climb into the wagon, and take up the reins. The leather straps feel heavy in my hands. Papa never used to let me drive the wagon. He said I was too small to hold Sadie back. I'm glad Moses is close by. He rides near the mule's head, flicking Papa's whip against her rump to keep her moving.

Solomon kneels in the back, watching until the bluff is out of sight. I keep my eyes on the ruts ahead. How can we leave Mama and Papa alone on this empty prairie?

Louisa sits next to me, whimpering to her ugly dried apple doll, telling it all about Mama and Papa's sickness. She looks up at me, her face streaked with crying. "It's not fair," she says. "How come you're the only one with blue eyes, like Mama?"

I bite my lip. I'd never thought of that before. I hold the reins in one hand and put my arm around Louisa. "But you have Grandma's pretty gray eyes," I tell her.

"I can't remember what she looks like."

I try to imagine Grandma sitting next to us. "She's heavy and short, like Mama." Solomon wiggles in next to me on the wagon seat, his thumb deep in his mouth, listening. "And she has a bubbly laugh. She keeps some noisy geese." I imagine Grandma filling the doorway of her cabin, her silver hair coiled on top of her head.

"Where does Grandma live?" Solomon asks.

I think about the route Papa made us memorize. "On the banks of the Little Sandy River," I say. I try to smile at them. "Grandma will be so happy to see us."

"Even without Mama?" Louisa's voice quivers.

"Of course." But I wonder.

Before I can dream up more worries, Moses stops Ginger suddenly, blocking the trail.

"Whoa!" I pull up on Sadie's reins. We've reached the crossroads near a ferry landing, but Moses has turned his mare the wrong way, headed upstream. His shoulders are shaking. I jump into the muddy track, grab the mare's bridle, and peer up into his face. "Moses, what's wrong?"

"Let's go back, Jess. We can use Papa's money to buy better land, or travel west with Mr. Flower, the man I met at English Prairie." Moses pulls his hat down to cover his red eyes. "It's a long way to Kentucky. I don't know if we can make it."

I stand on tiptoe, keeping my voice low. "You promised Papa you'd take us home. You swore on the Bible!"

"I know." Moses turns away. "Maybe I'll break my promise."

"You can't!" I stomp my foot. "We're going home, to Grandma—"

Suddenly, Solomon calls in a shrill voice, "Here comes a boat!"

I whirl around. A small ferryboat drifts down river, with a cabin set on the back. There are two men on deck, poling the boat forward with long oars, and a man in the back, steering. Solomon jumps to the ground and runs to the landing, bouncing up and down. "Boatman! Boatman!" he cries. "Over here!"

"Solomon, stop!" Moses calls.

I rush to catch hold of Solomon before he tumbles off the dock. "Bring me Papa's money," I call to

Moses. "I'm taking the little ones home." Solomon, Louisa, and I scream and yell until the man steering the boat sees us at last. He leans on his tiller and the boat's prow turns toward us across the current.

⚓ 9 ⚓

Danger on the Wabash

June 28, 1828.

Down the Wabash River to Shawneetown, Illinois.

The tillerman is tall, with a ruddy face and a gleaming bald head. "Someone catch the line," he calls. When Moses holds back, I run forward and the man in the prow tosses me a heavy rope. "Too weak to help, son?" the prow man jeers at Moses. Moses hurries over with a red face and loops the rope around a post.

"Where are you young ones headed?" the tillerman asks.

"Shawneetown," I tell him.

"Wagon and animals going, too?" he asks. "That's a lot of weight."

"We have money." I give Moses a look. His mouth is tight, but he reaches into his pocket to pay the pilot, the man at the tiller.

As we lead Sadie to the boat, a burlap sack on the deck wriggles and a silky brown head pokes out.

"A puppy!" Louisa squeals. She lifts her skirts and jumps onto the deck. Solomon follows her. They untie the sack and free the dog. It's the color of hazelnuts, with white splashes on its chest. Its ears are so long, it almost trips on them as it wiggles into Louisa's arms. She clutches it to her chest, and the puppy licks her chin, its tail circling in a blur.

The pilot laughs. "That's two who decided to get on board," he says. "Come on, load up the rest."

It takes everyone to push the mule onto the boat. Sadie stiffens her legs. She tosses her head and bucks, even with Moses clucking and singing to her. Finally, a man with a droopy mustache takes Papa's willow whip and snaps it near her rump. She jumps onto the boat, nearly tipping the wagon. When she's hobbled and tied to the railing and the wagon is lashed to the deck, the boatman beckons to Moses. "Bring that horse now."

Moses moves so slowly, I can almost feel him leaning toward the western prairie, but he leads Ginger onto the deck as if he'd planned it all along. "Thanks," I whisper, as the boat eases back into the current. Moses shrugs, but he stays turned toward the landing we've left behind, even after we pass the first bend in the river.

"Will we sleep on the boat?" Solomon's brown eyes are wide with excitement. Before the pilot can answer, Solomon asks, "What kind of boat is it?"

The pilot laughs. "Full of questions, aren't you? It's called a broadhorn." He points to the oars. "See the way those oars stick up over the cabin, like horns on a steer? Guess that's how she got her name. Anyway, I built her myself. It's a small cargo boat—we'll pass some bigger ones, headed for the Mississippi. Some are eighty feet long."

Solomon lets go of the railing and stands on tiptoe beside the cabin, trying to see into the small round holes. "What are those for?"

The man with the mustache, rowing at the front of the boat, gives a nasty laugh. "That's where we shoot our guns, when we're ambushed."

Solomon runs back to me and clings to my skirt. The pilot laughs. "Don't worry. It's a short trip to Shawneetown—just a few hours downstream. We'll be there by nightfall—and I doubt we'll have any trouble."

We're moving faster now. We drift past clumps of willows, their long slender leaves trailing in the water. Mama always loved willows. My eyes burn. As if he can read my mind, the pilot calls out to me, "So, where are your folks?"

"We're going to visit our grandmother," Moses says, and pinches me so hard, I almost cry out. I don't dare look at him. I guess he doesn't want me to tell about Mama and Papa. I bite my lip. We should have made up a story together. I hope the little ones don't give us away.

But Solomon saves us. He cries out, "Look! Another boat!" Sure enough, a big boat, its long deck covered with wooden barrels, draws up behind us. The pilot shouts some nasty words at the crew and they lean over their oars, pushing us out of the way. I let out a deep breath. The pilot has forgotten his question.

The muddy current carries us downstream. Louisa sits on the deck, stroking the puppy. She feeds it crumbled johnnycake she had hidden in her skirt. "Can I keep it?" she begs.

"Ask the men," I say.

The man with the mustache has a cruel laugh. "Do what you want. We were ready to toss it in the river. That sack is full of stones."

Two pink spots shine on Louisa's cheeks. "You were going to drown it? That's *mean*."

Moses comes over and lifts the dog above his head. "A boy pup," he says. "Maybe he'll turn into a coon hound."

"Not likely," the boatman mutters.

Louisa's eyes are on Moses. "Can I have him?" she pleads. "Please? I'm going to name him Sandy, after Grandma's river."

Solomon pulls his thumb from his mouth and strokes the puppy's head. "Can we?"

I pluck Moses's sleeve. "Let them," I whisper. "The pup's an orphan, like us. And they need some comfort."

"All right," Moses says at last.

I wink at Louisa behind his back. She smiles for the first time since Mama died, showing gaps where her bottom teeth are missing. The puppy nestles into her lap.

"So," the prow man asks in his nasty voice, "where'd you say your folks were?"

This time, before Moses or I can answer, Solomon pipes up. "Mama and Papa died."

"*Orphans.*" The prow man almost spits out the

word. He calls to the man behind him. "Hey, Mike. You need some children to work your farm?"

Moses steps in front of us, his legs braced apart. Solomon clutches my skirt and Louisa begins to howl. "We're going to Grandma!" she sobs.

"Of course we are." I stroke her thin hair and turn on the prow man, trying to sound brave. "We're not to be bound out." I touch the bodice of my dress, to make sure the letter is still there.

"Is that so?" The prow man laughs.

"Roger," the pilot growls from the back. "Come to your senses. No one wants a litter of young ones, especially sniveling babies. Now, keep a look out for that sandbar."

"I'm not a *baby*," Solomon says. I whisper in his ear, telling him to hush. The prow man grumbles and turns his back. But we don't feel safe. We huddle together, stroking the puppy, as the Wabash carries us to Shawneetown.

⚔ 10 ⚔

Trapped

June 28, 1828.

Shawneetown, Illinois.

The pilot was right: No one wants ragged, dirty children who whimper and whine. By late afternoon, when the broadhorn pulls up to the landing, Louisa and Solomon have worn us out with their crying. The nasty prowman looks the other way when Louisa tucks the puppy into her shawl. "Good riddance," he grumbles.

Shawneetown is a busy settlement with hundreds of log cabins jumbled near the river. As Moses hitches up the mule, the pilot takes me aside. "This town is too rough for children," he says. "Keep a tight hold on the little ones, and stay with my friend Willie Cottland. He lives outside of town, near the saltworks. You'll be safe there."

Even though the pilot was rough with his crew, his brown eyes seem kind now. I hope we can trust him.

Moses puts the little ones up on Ginger's back and lets me lead her while he drives the wagon. The streets are full of people yelling, pushing, and shoving their way to the docks. We pass a bank, a newspaper office, a blacksmith's shop—even a shoemaker. I peer into his window. If only I could slip a pair of soft boots over my cold, cracked toes!

"Can I have money for shoes?" I ask Moses, but he's following the smell of fresh bread from the bakery next door. Papa would have bought me shoes, I think, but Papa's gone. Besides, my stomach is empty, so I don't protest when Moses hands me some pennies and sends me inside to buy bread.

The baker is just setting new loaves on a wooden counter. I stand behind a thin woman, my stomach growling so loud, I'm afraid she'll hear it. When it's my turn to choose, the baker looks down his nose at me. "Didn't your mama tell you to wash before you eat?"

I keep my head up, even though my cheeks are hot. I won't tell him I have no mama to scold me or keep me clean. Instead, I buy five warm rolls and bring them outside. We sit in the wagon and gobble them down, feeding the extra one to the puppy.

I lick the crumbs from my fingers and look at Moses. He nods. "It won't hurt us to have another one," he says. "We can't let the little ones go hungry."

"You go in," I say. I'm ashamed of my dirty hands and face now. Moses comes out with two more rolls for each of us, but his face is dark and he makes us eat fast. When our bellies are as round and full as the pup's, Moses moves us all down the street and draws us close together in the wagon. "That baker was pestering me with questions," he says. He takes Louisa and Solomon's hands. "Listen carefully," he says. "You can't tell anyone that Mama and Papa died."

Solomon's lip trembles. "Why not?"

I pull him into my lap. "Because we might get bound out," I say. "And we'd never get home to Grandma."

"What's 'bound out'?" Louisa asks.

"It's like being a servant," Moses explains, "except you can never leave. People who bind you out keep you until you're grown."

Louisa shivers. "I don't want to be bound out," she whispers.

"Of course not," Moses says. "So, if anyone asks, just say we're going home to our folks in Kentucky. That's not really a lie. Grandma is like folks. Understand?"

The little ones nod but they look confused. I wonder if they can keep such a big secret.

"We have to find some water to clean our faces," I say. "Otherwise, it looks as though we don't have any folks at all." We follow a side street to the riverbank and walk upstream from the ferry dock to wash our hands and faces. The Wabash doesn't seem very clean here, but at least we get the streaks and smudges off our cheeks.

A few blocks from the river, we ask a kindly woman the way to Mr. Cottland's place. She points to a plume of smoke in the distance. "See that smoke?

That's where they're stoking the fires for the salt kettles. He lives about a mile down that road." She smiles.

"Thank you, ma'am," I remember to say. I feel warm inside as we turn away. "Some folks are still nice," I say to Moses.

He grunts, but his eyes are dark. "Feels like we can't trust anyone," he says.

After many twists and turns, we come to a two-story house set back from the road with a rough sign nailed to its split-rail fence. "What's that say?" Moses asks.

"Rooms to let," I tell him. The house is made with real boards instead of logs. Chickens scratch in the yard. At the same moment, we all notice a tall boy with dark skin hoeing a patch of soil near the door.

Moses backs his mare away from the gate. "Stop the wagon," he tells me in a low voice. "Papa wouldn't let us stay at a slave house."

"But this is Illinois," I remind him.

The boy has heard us. He stops his work, leans on his hoe, and waves. "Howdy. Y'all need a room?"

Before we can answer, Solomon calls out from the wagon, "Are you a slave?"

"Solomon!" I gasp.

The boy gives Solomon an easy smile. "Don't worry—ain't no slavery here in Illinois. Don't you know that? My daddy bound me out last year." He draws himself up tall. "When I reach twenty-one, Mr. Cottland will give me a suit of Sunday clothes, a Bible, and a feather bed."

"You're bound out?" Louisa asks. She clutches my skirt.

The boy nods, then glances nervously over his shoulder as the door opens and a bent man with a scraggly beard peers out. "We got overnight company, George?" He looks us up and down. "Evening," he says. "I'm Mr. Cottland."

I stare. The old man's eyes are strange: One is gray, the other brown—and the gray eye turns in toward his nose. I glance at Moses. He shrugs, although he looks worried. I guess he's thinking what I am: We're tired and hungry, with nowhere else to go. Besides, the pilot said we'd be safe here.

"How much for a room?" Moses asks at last.

"Same as the taverns in town," Mr. Cottland tells us. "Twenty-five cents apiece for the night, with meals. Fifty cents for each horse, with feed. No charge for the baby."

"I'm not a *baby!*" Solomon protests. "I'm this many!" He holds up four fingers, the way Mama showed him to do.

"Hush." I stroke his tangled curls while Moses pulls coins from his pocket and counts out the money.

The old man cackles like one of his hens. "You children traveling alone with all kinds of money? Bit dangerous, ain't it?"

Moses glances at his boots, where the rest of the money is hidden, then quickly snaps his head back up. Did the old man notice? My hands go as cold as my feet as Mr. Cottland takes Moses by the elbow and leads him away. "I'll show you where to bed your animals."

"Y'all come on inside," says George.

We're trapped. The little ones clutch my hands. Are we crazy, to stay here?

⊰ 11 ⊱
'Tetched in the Head'

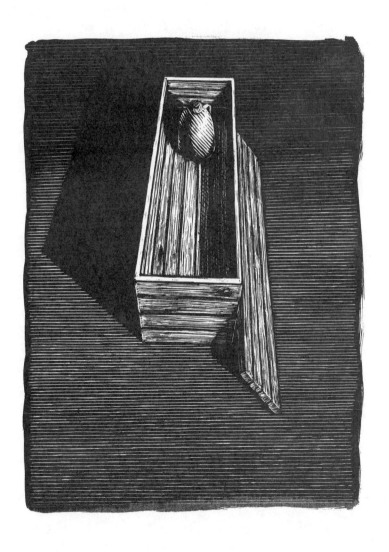

June 28–29, 1828.

Outside of Shawneetown, Illinois.

The puppy isn't worried about Mr. Cottland or his house. Sandy chases a cat right inside, and Solomon and Louisa race after him. I follow them into the front room. A shank of meat, sizzling on a spit over the fire, makes my mouth water. The kitchen has a puncheon floor made of new wood and a rocking chair that makes me think of Mama. The little ones plop down on the floor to play with Sandy, but I can't settle. I peer into a wooden bowl sitting on the plank table. It's full of peeled turnips, waiting to be boiled.

"Does Mr. Cottland have a wife?" I ask.

George laughs. "No. But he's always wishing he had some women around the house. 'Specially when I do the cooking." I have butterflies in my stomach.

Will Mr. Cottland try to keep Louisa and me here? As George leans over the fire, turning the meat on the spit, I ask, "Did you *choose* to be bound out?"

" 'Course not." He lowers his voice. "It's almost like being a slave. But what else could my daddy do? He couldn't feed us all. And I'm learning carpentry," he adds. "Come see what we've made."

He leads me across the hall into a dark parlor. I take a step forward and my hair prickles at my collar. Is that what I think it is? A long, empty coffin sits on the rag rug, its lid propped open.

"It's oak," George says. "With dovetail joints."

All at once, I picture Mama lying in her pine box, and Papa wrapped in the quilt. My head spins, and I stumble out of the room, breathing hard. George follows and I close the door behind us. Thank goodness Solomon and Louisa didn't see. George wrinkles his brow. "Sorry. I didn't mean to spook you," he says.

I shrug, as if I'm used to seeing empty coffins in parlors. When I finally find my voice, I ask, "Who died?"

"Nobody." He laughs. "Mr. Cottland built it for himself. He's crazy—'tetched in the head,' as my mama says. Keeps a jug of whiskey in there, 'case he gets thirsty on the way to heaven."

"Whew," I say. "That sure *is* crazy." I wipe my hands on my dress. This place is even spookier than I thought.

I don't tell the others what I've seen, but I'm testy all through dinner. I can't get Moses alone; he's too busy eating second portions of roast pork and mashed turnips. And when Mr. Cottland suggests we all have a bath, Moses agrees before I can even protest. "Saturday is bath night at our house, too," he adds. "Right, Jesse?"

Our house. I nod, but I'm all mixed up inside. Moses talks as if Mama and Papa were still alive! I guess he's trying to pretend we're not orphans. I help George and Mr. Cottland draw the extra water and heat it, keeping an eye on the closed parlor door.

Louisa and I have the first bath in the tin tub. When my sister strips off her clothes, her ribs look as bumpy as Mama's old washboard. She smells like curdled milk. We haven't had a bath since we left Illinois.

"Don't stare at me!" she complains.

"I'm not. Turn around and I'll scrub your back." For a minute, I'm furious with Mama for leaving me. Mama would know how to make our sack of cornmeal last, how to make soups and stews to help the little ones grow right. I'm only twelve! How will I feed everyone?

When I climb into the tub, wearing nothing but Papa's ring on its leather strap, it's Louisa's turn to stare. "You have bumps on your chest," she says.

"Go away," I snap.

Her eyes fill. "I want Mama," she says.

"So do I." I pull her into a wet, slippery hug.

I bathe and dry off as fast as I can. I'm ashamed I only have one clean pair of bloomers and one extra chemise to put on. My dress feels shabby and tight when I button it, and my feet still look filthy in spite of my scrubbing. I try to comb the snarls from Louisa's hair but she pulls away, yelping like the puppy. "You don't do it right!" she wails.

I give up. I'll never be able to fix things the way Mama could.

Moses and Solomon bathe next. When it's Mr. Cottland's turn, I hurry everyone out to the barn. "We're leaving," I tell them.

"But it's dark," Louisa whines. "I want to sleep here."

Moses slings his boots over his shoulder and pulls me aside. "What are you talking about? We paid good money to stay."

"That's all right. We're clean, and we had a good supper." I keep my voice low so the little ones won't hear me. "Listen. Mr. Cottland has an empty coffin sitting in his parlor, with a jug of whiskey inside. What if he gets drunk and puts one of us in there?"

Moses moves so fast, you'd think another panther was after us. In a few minutes, we've bundled Louisa and Solomon into the wagon, set the mule in her traces, and saddled Ginger. "Why are we going?" Solomon whispers.

"Hush," I tell him. "Do you want to be bound out, like George?"

Moses and I walk the animals slowly across the yard. Every squeak of the wheels makes my heart thump. As Moses opens the gate, we hear soft footsteps along the fence. I freeze. George pops out of the shadows, a bundle under his arm. "Take me with you," he begs.

"We can't," I whisper.

Solomon tugs my arm. "Why not?" he asks. "George is nice."

"Of course he is." I cover Solomon's mouth gently

with my hand to keep him quiet. "We're headed for Kentucky," I tell George.

"A *slave* state?" He drops his bundle on the ground. "I thought y'all were better than that." He melts back into the dark without saying good-bye.

"Wait!" I whisper. I want to explain, but Moses grabs my arm. "Get in," he says. "He might tell the old man."

I climb into the wagon, slap Sadie's rump with the reins, and turn her toward the rising moon. She trots to keep up with Ginger. George's words make my cheeks burn, but what else can we do? We promised Papa we'd find our way home.

It won't be so easy. The next night, long after we've crossed the Ohio River and celebrated our return to Kentucky, Moses discovers the money is missing from one of his boots. Even worse, I've left Papa's letter on the puncheon floor of Mr. Cottland's house.

⚜ 12 ⚜

Runaway Wagon

June 30, 1828.

On the road to Henderson, Kentucky.

"How could you!" Moses shouts that night, when I tell him what happened. "That letter was the most important thing Papa gave us!"

"What about the money?" I cry. "How could *you* leave your boots where crazy Mr. Cottland could find them?"

"What was I supposed to do?" Moses's voice breaks. "Take them into the tub with me?" For some reason, this makes us both laugh, even though we're in a lot of trouble now. Moses sighs. "At least he only robbed one boot—and I have a little money in my pocket, left over from the last ferry." He wrings his hands. "I guess we were both spooked by that place."

"*I* sure was. Why would anybody keep a coffin in

87

their parlor?" I shiver, and then I think of something embarrassing. What if George finds my dirty chemise lying in a heap on the floor? "At least we caught that first ferry out this morning. And we've come too far for him to chase after us."

Moses counts out the rest of our money. "Twenty-nine dollars—plus two Spanish piasters. We have to make it last. I'll try to shoot more game."

"We could always sell the silver stock on Grandfather's gun."

Moses shakes his head. "Not yet. Papa would never forgive us. We'll just have to be extra careful. And no more staying with strangers, especially without the letter."

I wave my hand around the dark clearing. "No one will bother us here." Giant oaks and black walnut trees tower over us. Even though the sky is still gray high above the trees, there's no light on the forest floor. The woods are full of spooky sounds: branches snapping, coyotes yipping, and an owl hooting.

Moses grips the rifle on his knees. "I don't like this place. It feels like a cave." He leans close to me. "What if we never make it to Grandma's?"

I turn on him, fast. "Don't talk that way! Of course we will." But I'm just as worried as he is. We haven't heard from Grandma in so long. Besides, she's old. What if she can't take care of us?

We travel along the road to Henderson, then Hardensburg, for five days, following Papa's directions. It's a dusty road, but well made. There are bridges instead of fords over some of the creeks. Little groups of people and animals pass, but they're all hurrying west, driving pigs, cows, and even a flock of geese down the muddy track. "Where are they going?" I ask.

"Out to the prairies," Moses says. "Guess they've heard land is only five dollars an acre." His face is sad as he watches them go, but he kicks up Ginger with his heels. Seems like he's given up his dream of heading west, at least for now.

Mr. Cottland's tin tub seems a long way back. Our clothes are muddy, my hands are blistered from holding the reins, and our supplies are running low. One night, Moses shoots a hare, and we feast on rabbit stew, but the next day, we're back to johnnycake again. My suppers are sometimes scorched, sometimes raw, but no one dares to complain.

When Solomon's face is all swollen from mosquito bites, I remember that last day at our cabin, helping Mama pack her herbs. I find the burdock in her box, set it in the herb crusher, and roll the wooden spindle back and forth to crush the leaves. Then I rub it on Solomon's skin to stop the itching, but it doesn't help, and he starts to weep for Mama. Soon Louisa joins in. I don't let myself cry. My heart aches too much. I'm afraid I'd never stop.

Six days from Shawneetown, we finally burst out of the woods. I'm so happy to see the open sky, I don't notice the steep pitch below us until the mule starts trotting. The wheels rumble and slide on the dry ruts. "Slow down!" Moses shouts. He's up ahead on the mare.

"Whoa!" I yell, yanking back on the reins. The wagon bucks and lurches too fast down the hill. Solomon and Louisa scream, and the puppy yips. Moses jumps off Ginger and grabs Sadie's bridle as she canters past. She jerks her head, dragging him along. "Grab the brake!" Moses yells.

Louisa and Solomon lean back on the wooden brake, but their spindly arms aren't strong enough to stop the clattering wheels. I grip the reins tight. "Moses, let go! She'll crush you!"

He turns and lunges for the wagon, catching the brake. His eyes bug out like a grasshopper. He braces his body against the wheel as I haul on the reins. "Watch out!" I scream.

An ox cart lumbers toward us, filling the road. Sadie swerves to the side. The wagon scrapes a tree and nearly tips over. Sadie squeals and kicks, caught in the traces. The wagon stops, wedged between two trees.

Louisa and Solomon are screaming. I pull them from the wagon and run to Moses. He's crouched in the road, his face streaked with axle grease, gripping his ankle. "The wheel ran over my foot. Find Ginger," he moans.

But the mare is gone and Moses is badly hurt. I stare at my brother, afraid if I touch his bleeding ankle, I'll make it worse. I bite my lip, to keep from crying out for Mama. Moses is the oldest, the one who takes care of us. If he can't walk, how will we go on?

13
Captured!

June 30, 1828.

On the road to Hardensburg,

in western Kentucky.

As I bend down to help my brother, we hear shouts. "Hold on! Help is coming!"

A short, bowlegged man trundles toward us. He clucks over Moses like an angry hen, then pokes his ankle. Moses cries out, but the man says, "Not broke; just sprained, with a nasty cut. We'll help you, lad." He points at me. "Take his other side."

Moses drapes one arm over my shoulder, the other over the man's, and we lift him up. I turn toward our wagon, but the man shakes his head. "Put him in my cart. Cabin's just down the road. Martha will fix him."

Is this man safe? There's no time to worry about that now. Moses sits on the back of the cart, his leg propped up, while the man and I back Sadie out from between the trees. Solomon yanks his thumb from his mouth. "The devil!" he cries, pointing at the man.

"Solomon!" I scold him. "Don't be rude." But I see what Solomon means. Everything about the man is red: his bushy hair and beard, his shirt and cheeks, even his suspenders.

The man laughs. "Don't worry, lad. I'm just old Henry Smith. Martha and I will get you out of this fix."

The wagon works in spite of a broken spoke. Just beyond the ox cart, we find Ginger, her eyes wild, her ears flat against her head. "Easy, girl," Moses calls. I hand him the reins and he keeps a tight hold as Ginger trots after the cart.

"We're going the wrong way," Louisa says suddenly.

I look down at her, surprised. "Aren't you smart!" I stroke her hair. "But don't worry. Moses will rest his foot, and then we'll get back on the trail." I don't tell her how nervous I am, going to a stranger's house without Papa's letter.

The Smiths' log house sits at the edge of the woods. The logs of the cabin are cut square, instead of rounded like trees, and chinked with mud. A little field of tobacco grows in the hollow at the foot of the hill. The rows of plants zig and zag around rotten tree stumps. The broad green leaves, shining against the black soil, make me think of Papa's corn, and how it never came up right.

Mr. Smith whistles and his wife comes out of the house. She's a tall, bony woman with big hands. When she sees us, a smile lights up her face. "You poor young ones!" Her voice trills up and down as she

94

fusses over us. She pulls off Moses's boots. I cover my mouth when I see his foot, to keep myself from crying out. It's all caved in where the wheel went over his ankle. While Mrs. Smith cleans his foot and wraps it in a poultice, Moses signals to me to keep the boots. I hold them tight to my chest.

"Do you have willow bark for the pain?" I ask.

Mrs. Smith's eyebrows shoot up. "What a clever girl. Who taught you about healing?"

"Mama," I say, and then clamp my mouth tight. I don't want any more questions.

I keep a close watch on the Smiths for the next hour, but it's different from Mr. Cottland's house. They make a fuss over us, treating us like special guests. Mrs. Smith heats a basin of hot water so we can wash our faces while Mr. Smith makes a crutch for Moses from an oak branch. Mrs. Smith draws Louisa into her lap, humming a little song and combing the nasty tangles out of her hair. Louisa doesn't even complain. Her eyes get dreamy and far away. She must remember the way Mama used to sing to us at night. I want to warn her not to get too close, but I can't say anything.

Later, the Smiths ladle out bowls of rabbit stew for everyone, even Sandy. The puppy licks his bowl clean, then pushes it across the hard-packed dirt floor with his nose, making us laugh.

After supper, Solomon's head droops against my shoulder. Mr. Smith lights his pipe. "So," he asks, between puffs, "y'all going to like sleeping in our boat tonight?"

Solomon's head jerks right up again. "A boat?" he asks. "Where?"

Mr. Smith chuckles. "Right here. This cabin was a longboat. Martha and me, we sailed it down the Ohio. When we landed, we took the boat apart, hauled the logs in here, and made us a house. Only thing missing is children. Right, Martha?"

She nods. Her eyes are nearly closed, but I can feel her squinting at us through those tiny slits. I glance at Moses, but he's asleep in the corner, his boots under his head. Mrs. Smith clears her throat and asks the question we all dread. "Where are your Mama and Papa?"

Louisa's eyes fill with tears. "They died," she whimpers. I dig into her ribs with my elbow and she claps a hand over her mouth, horrified. "I mean—"

"We're going to Grandma's," Solomon says in a brave voice, but it's too late.

"Poor little lambs." Mrs. Smith gives her husband a funny look. He sucks on his corncob pipe and nods. An icy chill slides down my spine.

"I'm sorry," Louisa whispers later, when I settle her and Solomon on a pallet next to the fire. "She was being nice. Like Mama. I forgot."

"Don't worry," I tell her. But I *am* worried. I only pretend to sleep while the Smiths talk.

"Orphans," Mrs. Smith whispers. "The answer to my prayers."

Mr. Smith grunts. "Mebbe," he says. "But we cain't feed four."

"Just the little ones," she says. "Please, Henry. Think of the two babes we lost. It's like God brought them back to us."

I open my eyes enough to see his big hand cover hers on the table. "Very well," he says. "We'll bind the young ones to us, and send the others away. That girl's a bit snippy anyhow."

Snippy? I clench my fists. Why should I be polite to someone who's trying to steal my brother and sister?

"What if they won't leave the little ones?" Mrs. Smith whispers.

He chuckles. "Don't worry. When I bedded their animals, I took the boy's rifle."

I grit my teeth. I won't let them steal Louisa and Solomon. And Grandfather's rifle? With the silver stock? They can't have that either.

I'm too mad to cry. I cup my hand around Papa's ring. *Papa*, I whisper to myself. *Help me.*

As if he's heard me, I suddenly know what to do.

14

The Trick

June 30, 1828.

Near Hardensburg, Kentucky.

I wait until the Smiths are both snoring on their narrow pallet. One of them sounds like a kettle whistling. I inch out from under the quilt and slip Mama's diary, quill pen, and ink bottle from my leather pouch. I lie close to the fire, squinting to see in the dim light of the flames licking the back log. I try to remember Papa's words, just as he recited them to me.

To my fellow Masons, I write. The pen makes a scritching sound on the paper. I stop, holding my breath. The snoring goes on, like two cats purring. I dip the quill into the ink bottle, writing carefully. If only I'd read the letter again! But I remember the most important part:

My children travel home to their grandmother on the Little Sandy River. Please give them safe passage. They are not to be bound out . . . I stop. There was something about "protection," but I don't know how to spell such a big word, so I skip over that part. *I swear a solum oath on the Bible that these words, in my daughter's hand, are my own.* I read it over carefully, my hands shaking. That word *solum* looks funny.

I leave the diary open to dry the ink, and stand up slowly. Sandy's tail thumps. I stroke his long ears until he dozes off, then edge to the table in the middle of the room, my hand groping for the candlestick.

Bang! The candlestick falls over. I catch it before it rolls off the table. My heart pounds. Mr. Smith snorts, and Mrs. Smith murmurs, "Whassat?"

"A log popping," he grumbles.

I don't move a muscle. It seems like hours before they're both snoring again. Finally, I carry the candle to the fire, hold the wick to the coals to light it, and let the wax drip gently onto the paper. I spit on my fingers, pinch out the flame, then press Papa's ring into the soft wax. I even remember to sign his initials, W. J. D., just the way he did. Should I tear the pages from the diary?

No—too noisy. Instead, I hold the book open to the fire until the ink is dry, then curl up with the book under my arm. Papa told me to be as tough as my grandfather. *Okay Papa,* I think. *I've done my best.*

I hardly sleep a wink, and I'm up before the Smiths, packing our small bundles when the sky is barely gray.

"Why, Jesse," Mrs. Smith says, her voice drippy as sorghum. "Where are you off to so early?"

"We have to be on our way, ma'am." I can fake a sweet voice as well as she can. "Our grandma is waiting on us."

"Is that so?" Mr. Smith swings his feet over the edge of the bed, pulling his suspenders over his bare chest. "We have a little surprise for you."

I hear a stumbling noise behind me. I know Moses is nearby, but I don't dare look at him. I clutch Mama's book under my arm.

"You and your brother may do as you like," Mr. Smith says. "But me and Martha, here, we thought we'd keep the little ones with us. Give them a good home."

"No you won't!" Moses lurches past me, forgetting his ankle, then cries out and plops onto a stool. His face is gray as the cold ashes on the hearth. As he doubles over, I dig my fingers into his shoulder.

"We can't be bound out." Somehow, my voice stays calm, even though my palms are so wet, I'm afraid I'll drop the book. "We have a letter here, from our Papa. He wrote it before he died. Didn't he?" I give Moses a tight smile.

Moses rubs his eyes, looking confused. "Why— yes," he says at last.

Before Moses can ask me what I'm doing, I open the diary and hand it to Mr. Smith. He squints at it, holding it on his round belly. "Don't look like a man's hand to me," he says.

"Papa dictated it to me." I point to the wax. "That's his seal. He couldn't read or write."

"Same as me." Mr. Smith shoves the diary toward

his wife. "You puzzle it out, Martha." Mrs. Smith reads the way Louisa does, whispering the words to herself. "Read it so I can hear," Mr. Smith says.

Mrs. Smith holds the letter up close and reads out loud. She trips over the word *solum,* but she seems to know what it means. When she's finished, she looks at us, then at Mr. Smith. Tears roll down her cheeks. I hold my breath, not daring to look at Moses, waiting to hear what she'll say.

✄ 15 ✄

Where's Solomon?

June 30–July 6, 1828.

Near the Ohio River.

Mrs. Smith wipes her tears. "My daddy was a Mason, too. He took a vow to help those in need, especially widows and orphaned children." She looks at Mr. Smith. "Their papa asks his Mason friends to give the children safe passage. We have to let them go."

I want to dance a jig and whoop like an old screech owl, but instead I keep a sugary smile pasted on my face and say—ever so careful not to look at Moses— "We thank you for your kindness, ma'am." And then, as sweet as can be, I point to the gun, propped beside their pallet. "That looks like our grandfather's Kentucky rifle—the one the government gave him for bravery."

Mr. Smith's face turns as red as his hair. "Yes—

uh, you're right," he stammers. "I was fixing to clean it for you. It's a beauty. Your grandfather must have been a good man."

Even though my heart is beating like partridge wings, I nod like nothing is wrong and thank him, too.

Later that morning, we leave with our bellies full of porridge, the rifle clean and polished, and a new wheel spoke. As we draw away from the cabin, Mr. Smith calls out, "Keep your eye out for canebrakes— there's good feed for the animals in there."

Moses waves and slaps Sadie's rump with the reins. His foot hurts too much to ride Ginger, so he's sitting beside me on the seat while the mare trots behind, her reins hitched tight to the wagon. The minute we turn onto the trail, Moses and I howl with laughter. Louisa and Solomon scramble forward.

"What's so funny?" Louisa asks.

"Your sister really fooled those people," Moses says, nearly choking. When he can speak, he explains how I faked a copy of Papa's letter.

Louisa squeezes between us on the seat. "Did they want to steal us?"

"They did. But Jesse was too smart for them."

My cheeks feel warm. I'm not used to hearing praise from Moses.

Louisa looks up at me, puzzled. "But they seemed nice. Mrs. Smith sang to me, like Mama."

"And they live in a boat," Solomon says.

Louisa buries her head on my shoulder. "I didn't mean to tell about us being orphans," she says.

I pat her knee. "I know. Just be careful next time."

Moses frowns. "I think we should say we're meeting our folks in the next town. For today, that's Hardensburg." He looks over his shoulder at Solomon. "Can you remember that?"

Solomon nods, but he pokes his thumb into his mouth.

A week later, we're creeping along a ridge trail, trying to escape the mud in the valleys. It's been raining for two days. We're all cranky, especially Moses. Even though it's hot, we've pulled quilts and blankets around our heads to keep the mosquitoes away. Our cornmeal is wet, and every time we try to make a fire, we get lots of smoke but not enough heat for cooking.

As Sadie struggles to pull the wagon, a green bird flies over us, squawking. Solomon peeks out from under his blanket. "What was that?"

Louisa points. "Look—it's coming back!" The bird swoops through the trees. It's as big as a crow, with a bright yellow head. Sadie shies and stomps when it squawks again. "What is it?" Louisa asks. The bird lights on a branch just up the trail. It twists its head to the side. Louisa laughs. "It's watching us! Can we catch it and keep it? Please?"

"Don't be foolish," Moses says.

Louisa's face crumples up and I scowl at Moses. "That was mean," I tell him. I watch the bird. It flies ahead of us a way, then stops to wait. "Seems as if it's trying to tell us something," I say.

At that moment, we all hear the noise. It sounds like a tornado wind—but the trees stand still in the soft drizzle. As the wagon inches forward, the sound grows louder, until it's almost a roar. My stomach is clenched up. I think we should turn and run, but I want to see what it is, at the same time.

"Whoa!" Moses yells. He draws Sadie up on the edge of a bluff. The Ohio River is down below, all muddy and churned up. The noise is coming from a foaming chute in the river. As we stare with our mouths open, a big broadhorn bobs on the current, headed straight for the rapids. A tiny group of men and women are bunched together on the deck. We're too far away to see their faces, but we can hear them screaming. Solomon stands behind me, his nails digging into my shoulders. "They're going to drown!" he cries.

I hold my breath. The boat shoots into the center of the rapids and almost disappears, as if there's a deep trough in the middle. The prow rises up, then the stern. The boat seems to bounce and then it pops out of the rapids as if it was shot from a slingshot. The people are still standing on the deck as the crew poles the broadhorn into the slower current and the boat keeps on downstream.

"I'm glad we're not on *that* ferry," I say.

Suddenly, Solomon screeches as if he's been stung, jumps from the wagon, and runs to the edge of the bluff, screaming and pointing. "Look! Another boat! It's on fire!" We hurry after him. A huge boat, with two smoking chimneys, steams down the muddy river toward a landing above the rapids. "What is it?" Solomon asks.

"A steamboat." Moses's eyes are as big as Solomon's. "Papa told me about them. The fire makes that big wheel turn and run the boat."

"Can we ride it?" Solomon asks.

Moses shakes his head, but he's got that same dreamy look he had when he told me about the western prairies. "It's headed the wrong way. We need to save our money to buy food in Louisville. The salt pork is gone, we're almost out of cornmeal, and I can't hunt with my foot hurt so bad."

Solomon starts to cry, and the rain falls harder, as if the sky is crying, too. I take a deep breath. "If we sold Ginger, we'd have enough money to ride a boat up the river." I feel mean, even thinking of this, but my stomach growls, reminding me we need food. "Besides, you can't ride Ginger until your foot is better."

Moses looks hurt. "Ginger's *my* mare. I raised her from when she was a foal. And I won't be lame forever."

His ankle is still swollen, as if he stepped into a nest of yellow jackets. I wonder if he'll ever walk right again, but of course I don't say so. I know why he doesn't want to give up Ginger. I remember how I felt about losing Nettie.

"Ginger eats more than the mule," I say at last. "We don't have enough oats for both of them."

Moses's mouth is set so straight, he looks like he caught Sadie's stubbornness. "Remember what Mr. Smith told us—that there's plenty of feed for horses in the canebrake."

I cross my arms over my chest, facing him. "But there's no cane here," I say, "and Sadie's going so slow in all this mud—what if we never get home?"

"Don't fight," Louisa begs. The puppy whimpers and licks my hand. Just then, two black plumes of smoke puff out of the chimneys and the boat eases into its landing.

Solomon tugs at Moses's belt with one small hand. "It's turning around. *Please,* can we ride on it?"

To my surprise, Moses pulls himself up and says, "All right. A boat will get us home faster than a poky mule. Come on, let's go down to the dock. Maybe someone on that steamer needs a good horse."

Before dark falls, we've sold Ginger to a man who's headed to Henderson. Ginger whinnies and snorts as the man leads her away. Louisa plugs her ears, and Moses pulls his hat down over his eyes. He shoves some money in my hand. "Buy us some tickets to Cincinnati," he tells me.

As the crew loads barrels, sacks, and crates on board, Moses studies our rough map. "We're leaving Papa's route," he says. "How will we find our way?"

"Don't worry," I say. "Someone on the boat will know how to find the Little Sandy River." The crowd pushes us toward the gangway. Sparks rain from the steamer's chimneys. Solomon bounces with excitement.

Moses ties his bandanna over Sadie's eyes so she won't see the boat. She still balks and prances as we pull her through the crowd. A whistle sounds so loud I clap my hands over my ears. When I uncover them, Louisa is tugging on my skirt. "Jesse!" she yells, "the puppy is gone!"

"He's not with you?"

Louisa shakes her head, biting her lip. The whis-

112

tle shrieks again, and she wails, almost as loud, "Where's Solomon?"

I shove through the crowd and rush to the railing, as the steamer chugs away from the shore. "Solomon!" I scream.

The only answer is the boat's piercing whistle.

16

Stop the Boat!

July 6, 1828.

On the Ohio River,

from Louisville to Cincinnati.

Moses, Louisa, and I hurry around the deck, knocking into passengers, tripping over bushel baskets and steamers trunks, searching for Solomon. The boat is as big as a mansion. How will we ever find him? We look under chairs, inside the cabin, behind coils of rope, under a lifeboat. Moses tells a sailor that our brother is missing, and pretty soon lots of people are shouting "So-o-ol-omon!"

I grip the railing, gasping for breath. The landing is a shadowy line in the distance, and the river swirls behind the churning paddle wheels. What if he's still on shore? Or worse—but I can't think about that. Solomon can't swim.

I crane my head to see the deck above me. A burly,

bearded man wearing a black cap and a brass-buttoned jacket stands behind a wheel, barking orders. Is that the captain?

"Sir!" I call, waving my arms, but he doesn't hear me. Without even thinking, I scramble up the steep stairs, lift my torn skirt, and climb over the railing until I'm right behind him. I tug on his sleeve and he whirls around.

"What on earth!" His scowl is fierce. He beckons to a boatman nearby. "Carl—get this young urchin off my bridge."

Urchin! I'm boiling inside, but I force myself to stay polite, meeting the man's steely blue eyes. "Sir, my little brother is lost. I'm afraid we might have left him on shore." I take a deep breath. "Please stop the boat!"

He shakes his head. "I'm the captain, and the *Elizabeth Ann* doesn't stop for anyone. Tell your folks to take better care next time."

I swallow all my worries about our safety. I'd rather be bound out than have Solomon drown. "Sir, we don't have any folks. And my brother is only four years old. He's just a baby."

The captain curses under his breath, then yells, "Reverse engines!"

His command sends boatmen running up and down ladders, across the decks, and into the hold. The great boat shudders and belches steam, losing speed. The paddle wheels slow. As I peer over the railing, a small brown head pokes out of an open hatch on the lower deck.

"Sandy!" I race down the stairs and crawl on my hands and knees over a pile of grain sacks until I reach the puppy. He licks my face all over, as if he hasn't seen me in weeks. "Where's Solomon?" I ask.

Sandy leans into the hole, snuffling and wagging his tail. Solomon is crouched far below on a bale of cotton, shaking with sobs. He reaches up to me. "I can't get out!"

I lie on my belly and stretch out my arms, but the hole is too deep. "Climb on the bales, the way Sandy did," I tell him.

"They're too high," he wails.

Heavy footsteps clomp behind me. The captain pushes me aside, swings down into the hold, and hands Solomon up to me. When the captain clambers out, his face is red with rage. "Whoever let these children on board?" he grumbles. "Full ahead!" he yells to the mate on the bridge. "The child is found!" The boat swings up river again.

Solomon's tears stop instantly. "Are you the *captain?*" he whispers, as if this man were President Adams. He reaches his short arms out to the captain, pointing up at the wheel. "Can I drive the boat?" he begs.

The captain's mouth twitches into a smile behind his beard. Even this fierce man can't resist my brother's big brown eyes. He sighs, pushing back his cap. "All right, young man."

He carries Solomon up to the bridge and sets him on a box so he can reach the wheel. The captain lays his own wide hands over my brother's small ones and they steer the boat together.

"Look, Jess!" I can barely hear Solomon's tiny voice over the chuff of the engines. "I'm making it go!"

I smile, yet my eyes burn with tears. Mama and Papa would be so tickled if they could see Solomon now. It's not fair! They'll never watch any of us grow up.

The captain leans over to tell Solomon something. Thank goodness my brother is safe, because I feel weak and woozy all of a sudden. I send Moses to the bridge and thread my way through the crowd, ignoring their grumbling. "Troublesome children—you've made us late," one man mutters. I don't care. I curl up next to our bundles.

When Moses finds me later, my head is throbbing, and my teeth chatter like the spoons Papa used to play. "What's wrong?" he asks.

"Nothing," I say. "I'm just cold." He brings me a quilt, his eyes full of worry. I wrap up inside it, but nothing can warm me. I ache to the insides of my bones. Without even looking, I know my hands and feet must be as blue as Mama's eyes. It's fever and ague. And no Mama to cure me this time.

17
Lost

July 6–9, 1828.

A dark crossroads in Washington, Kentucky.

I don't remember much about the boat ride. It seems as if I lay on that deck forever, burning with fever or shaking with chills. I had nightmares and woke to find Solomon and Moses leaning over me, their faces growing huge, then shrinking to tiny dots. Once, I felt something cool on my face, and for a second I thought Mama had come back to soothe me. But it was only Louisa with a drippy rag, trying to help. I thanked her, even though I longed for Mama's firm hands.

Somehow, Moses got us off the boat in Cincinnati, in spite of his bad leg. All I remember are the crowds at the dock, and how Moses laughed when I jabbered about being bound out. "Don't worry, Jess," he said.

"No one wants a family with a cripple and two sick kids."

Two? I guess that's when I realized Louisa had the ague, too. I wanted to stand up and help her, but my arms and legs seemed filled with wet sand. I kept telling Solomon and Moses about Mama's medicines, but they couldn't hear me. Every bump of the wagon jolted my bones.

Now I wake from a bad dream and find we're stopped beside the road. It's dusk, and someone is crying. Louisa and Solomon are asleep. My chills are better, so I crawl to the wagon seat and find Moses sitting with the Bible open to Papa's map, wiping away tears with his shirt sleeve. "What's wrong?" I whisper.

"We're lost," he says. "Since we took that steamboat we're not on Papa's map anymore."

I climb onto the seat beside him and look around. We're in the middle of a small village. A few cabins are set back from the road behind a line of trees. "Where are we?" I ask.

"Someplace called Washington," Moses says. "That's what one lady told me."

Now I feel really confused. "Washington—where the president lives?"

"No, Jess." Moses talks to me slowly, as if I were Solomon's age. "We're still in Kentucky. We followed the main road here, after we crossed over from Cincinnati. I don't know where that Blue Lick place is, where we go into the mountains." He snaps the Bible shut and rubs his eyes. "I can't see this map in the dark, anyway. Don't know why I even try."

I hate it when Moses sounds like he's about to give up. Just then, we hear rough laughter from across the road. A door slams, and a man comes out of a tall white building. Lantern light glows from the open window. I squint, trying to make out the letters on the sign swinging in the wind. *"Broderick's Tavern,"* I read. "Could you ask in there? Maybe we're not too far away."

He shakes his head. "We're supposed to climb into the hills, remember? It's pretty flat here."

He waves his arm. Even in the dusk, I can see rolling fields, with something green growing on the other side of the trees. "Do you remember the trail we're supposed to be on?" I ask.

"I think the road from Lexington to Paris." Moses pushes his hat back. "All right—I'll go into the tavern and get directions. I just hope no one asks about our folks."

"It's my fault we're on the wrong road," I tell him. "I wanted to take the steamboat."

Moses finally smiles. "We *all* did, Jess. Solomon more than anyone. He can't wait to grow up and be a riverboat captain." He picks up his crutch and slides to the ground, landing on his good leg. He fixes his worried eyes on me. "With you sick, and me hurt—how will we make it?"

"Don't talk that way!" I cry, although I'm scared, too.

"I'm sorry. Watch the little ones until I get back." He hobbles to the tavern and disappears into the light of the open doorway.

I sit on the wagon seat a long time, my teeth chattering. I keep an eye on the tavern door, trying to stay awake. "Jesse!" Louisa's voice is like a kitten mewling. "I'm so thirsty!" I pour out water from our jug. Her hands shake and she spills half of it down her dress. I settle her back under the sheepskin, then cuddle up under my quilt, waiting and listening. I hear distant singing and laughing, but it's hollow, as if I'm under water. Where is my brother? Did someone steal him?

When I wake up, Moses's pallet is still empty. The tavern is dark and quiet, and stars prick the sky. I have to find him.

Somehow, I lower myself to the ground. I clutch the wagon and walk around it, holding on, until I realize I'm walking in circles. "I'm delirious," I whisper, and for some reason this makes me laugh, then cry. I fall to the ground and try to crawl on my hands and knees toward the tavern, but the ruts in the road get higher and higher, until they are like the hills Papa told us we'd have to cross. "Moses," I call, "I found the mountains."

Next thing I know, it's dawn, and I'm lying in the wet grass beside the road. I hear wagon wheels and a woman's voice crying out, "Stop!" A brown face leans over me and I'm scooped up in strong arms. I feel as light as a taffeta skirt. God is taking me to Mama and Papa, I think.

But I can't go yet. There's something I have to remember. Something very important. What is it? "Wait!" I cry. "Don't forget them." But who do I mean? And why is no one listening to me?

☀ 18 ☀

Rescue

July 10, 1828.

North Fork of the Licking River, Kentucky.

I dream Mama is singing to me, and wake up in a
four-poster bed, lying on feather pillows soft as
clouds. The song goes on. It's not Mama. The voice is
strong and husky. Someone sings, *"Wade in the
water . . . God's gonna trouble the water."* I turn my
head slowly. I'm in a bright room with pink flowers
stenciled on the walls, lacy curtains blowing at the
open windows, and a braided rug on the floor. The
ceiling seems as far away as the sky. Beside me, on
a small table, Papa's ring rests on Mama's diary.

I turn the other way and find Louisa asleep, her
face as pale as the linen sheet covering us. She's
wearing a clean cotton nightdress, just like the one I
have on. "Louisa, where *are* we?" I whisper. "Maybe

we've died and gone to heaven. We'll find Mama here, singing with the angels."

The singing stops. "Don't tell me you're still crazy with fever." A young girl, with skin the same dusky brown as the Ohio River, pops to her feet at the end of the bed. She shakes her head at me. "This might look like heaven to you, but it ain't for me," she says. "It's the Widow Hopkins's place. She's been taking care of y'all since she and my Uncle Roy found you lying in the road."

I close my eyes. I remember a kind, dark face— but nothing more.

"I'll tell Widow Hopkins you're awake," the girl says, heading for the door.

"Wait." I sit up quick, finally remembering. "My brother is still in the tavern." I throw off the covers and try to stand, but my legs buckle like thin twigs.

The girl rushes over, catching me before I hit the rug. "Where you going?" she scolds. "You cain't walk yet. You nearly died of fever. You're just lucky the Widow Hopkins has that special medicine. Otherwise, you and your sister be dead, for sure."

I'm not really listening. "Moses never came back." I struggle to get away, but her hands are strong, even though she's small.

"You settle down," she says, as if she were my older sister. "He's in the parlor, with the doctor. But didn't he feel foolish, when we found him conked out under a tree! That brother of yours sure had some liquor in the tavern."

Moses was *drinking?* I smile in spite of myself. "Thank goodness my pa didn't know about that." As the girl opens the door, I ask, "What's your name?"

"Emilia. But most folks call me Emmy. I know you're Jesse," she adds. "Your little brother asks for you every second."

Next time I wake up, Louisa is sitting in a chair and an older white woman with steady gray eyes is feeling my pulse. "Your fever's broken," she says. "That's a good sign. Let's give you another dose of medicine." She stirs a spoonful of powder into a glass of water. "This is cinchona bark," she says. "The Indians use it, in South America. It saved your life. Drink it down, now."

The medicine is so bitter it makes me gag. Mama never gave us anything that tasted this bad, but the woman's face is stern and I don't dare spit it out. I swallow it down and lean back against the pillows. I want to ask when I can get up, but I can't keep my eyes open.

Sometime later, Moses stumps in on matching crutches with a clean bandage on his foot. His hair is trimmed, and his old shirt is clean and patched. "Is that really you?" I ask, trying to smile.

"Yes, it's me, don't worry." He stands in the corner, as if he doesn't want to get too close. "Sorry I scared you, at the tavern. They gave me something called cider oil. It's a mix of cider and apple brandy. It's stronger than corn liquor, but they didn't tell me that until it was too late. I was sick as a dog." His face is bright red.

"That's all right." I sit up carefully. "What did they do to your foot?"

"Put a wooden splint on it. The doctor brought me some new crutches. He says some bones are crushed. I guess that Mr. Smith didn't know what he was talking about. I need to rest it a while—and I may always have a limp." He looks away. "I won't be much of a farmer now."

I feel terrible. If only I'd kept Sadie from bolting. Moses is staring out the window. I wonder what he sees. "They won't bind us out, will they?"

"I doubt it. They don't need more servants here," he says with a dry laugh. "Look."

I slip out of bed and grip the bedpost to steady myself. Moses pulls back the curtain. I gasp. I've never been up so high in a house. I can see across the valley to a river. I feel like a bird as I look down on a green pasture sprinkled with white sheep. Two bay-colored horses canter across a paddock near the house. "It's beautiful," I say. "Mama would love those sheep. Can we stay forever?"

"Don't be foolish." He takes me to the other window. "Look."

I hold onto his shoulder. Two rows of small, rough cabins, the size of the one we left on the Little Wabash, are scrunched together behind a brick barn. Smoke trails from the chimneys. Beyond the cabins, black men and women are bent over rows of tobacco in a long field. Some are on their hands and knees, others are hoeing the red-brown soil.

"Slaves," I whisper. An icy chill slides down my spine. "Emmy's a *slave?*"

Moses nods. "There are one hundred slaves here, all serving the Widow Hopkins. You still want to stay?"

"Of course not." My eyes burn, holding back tears. "I didn't realize. Thank goodness we didn't bring George with us."

Moses nods. "He's better off, bound out. At least he'll be free when he's grown. Papa always told me slavery was evil, Jess, but I didn't understand. Not until now."

My legs are wobbly. I sit on the end of the bed. "I'm glad no one will want us here. But Moses," I whisper, "with all of us so sick and feeble—how will we ever get home?"

✣ 19 ✣

The Long Scar

July 10–15, 1828.

North Fork of the Licking River, Kentucky.

The Widow Hopkins watches us all the time, making me feel funny. But she also spoils us while Louisa and I get strong. She gives us new clothes and presents, as if it were Christmas—except Mama and Papa could never give us a Christmas like this one. Louisa has a fancy doll with a china head. Solomon has a wooden boat on a string that he floats in the muddy branch of the Licking River, which winds along at the foot of the widow's fields. As for me, I have a real book to read, and soon, Emmy tells me, I'll have another surprise.

Meanwhile, Moses won't wear the linsey-woolsey shirt the widow gave him. "She acts like she owns us," he tells me later. Yesterday, he repaired the wagon and groomed Sadie until her coat shone. His leg is healing, and he's moving pretty fast on his crutches now. I can tell he's itching to be gone, but I'm almost happy I feel so weak. It means I can wake up in the pink flowered room a few more times, stare at that high ceiling and pretend I'm in heaven with Mama and Papa.

One morning, I come out on the porch and find Emmy waiting for me. "Let's go," she says. "My daddy says the surprise is ready."

She leads me to the cabins where the slaves live, behind the barn. I drag my feet, and not just because I'm too wobbly to hurry. I'm scared of what I'll see.

The cabins are mean and shabby; most are empty. A tall man sits outside on a cobbler's bench, polishing a pair of shiny brown boots. "Hey, Daddy," Emmy says. "Here's Jesse."

The man glances at my bare feet before he looks at my face. "I believe these will do you," he says.

"You made those for *me?*" I whisper.

Emmy nudges me. "Try them on."

I take them carefully in my hands, as if they were one of the widow's fine china cups. The leather is smooth and soft, the color of walnuts. I slip my bare feet inside and lace them tight. "Thank you," I tell Emmy's father. "They fit just right. How did you know?"

Emmy laughs. "You sleep sound when you're sick," she says. "That's when me and the Widow Hopkins measured your feet. You like them?"

"They're beautiful. I never had new shoes of my own before."

"Me neither," Emmy says in a low voice.

I look down, ashamed. Emmy's feet are as bare as her daddy's. Something twists inside me, like a rope turned around on itself. I unlace the boots and pull them off. "Here," I tell Emmy. "You take them. They'd fit you."

She glances at her father, her eyes afraid. "Am I allowed, Daddy?"

He frowns. "Of course not. If the foreman saw you in those new boots, you'd get a lashing for sure."

"Let me ask the Widow Hopkins," I say. "Please. My grandma will buy me some shoes when we get home." Of course, Grandma doesn't have that kind of money, but I don't say so.

Emmy's father stands, turns his back, and lifts his shirt. A long scar criss-crosses his spine. When he looks at me again, his eyes are scary. "That's what the whip does. You want Emmy to have scars like mine?" he asks.

I can hardly speak. "No sir," I whisper.

"Then you take those boots." He tucks in his shirt and pulls Emmy close. "On some plantations, they sell the children away from their parents. Emmy's mama and I been lucky so far. We've kept the family together. You don't want us to lose her, do you?"

I bite my lip, holding back the tears. He makes me think about my own mama and papa, lying under that big oak tree. "I'm sorry," I whisper. "It's not fair." I clutch the boots to my chest and stumble to the house, so mixed up I want to scream.

Later that afternoon, the Widow Hopkins calls Moses and me out onto the shady verandah, where it's cool. She sits straight on a wooden chair, her

139

hands folded in her lap. Moses stands beside me near the long windows, balanced on his crutches.

"I'd like you children to stay here with me," the widow says.

My throat feels tight and dry. "We're not—to be bound out," I stammer.

"You wouldn't be," she says in a tight voice. "I am fortunate to be a wealthy woman. I would adopt you, give you a comfortable life—and an education."

Education. That word is as sweet as flapjacks with honey. I remember the schoolhouse in New Harmonie, with the children running outside. I hear Papa's voice, before he died, making me promise I'd get an education—and teach the little ones, too. I think about having real book learning, about knowing how to spell words like *solemn* and *protection*. But what about swearing on the Bible, saying we'd take the little ones home? What would Papa say if he knew I was wearing boots made by a slave?

Just then, Solomon and Louisa run toward us, chasing the puppy. Sandy scrambles up the porch steps, nearly tripping on his ears, and they hurry after him, squealing with laughter. "Calm down, now," the widow says, but she smiles and beckons them to her side. The puppy flops onto the porch, his tail thumping. Solomon and Louisa stand on either side of the widow's chair, panting for breath. Their cheeks are pink, and Louisa even has some flesh on her bones. They never looked this well, even with Mama and Papa's care. Is it right to make them leave?

The widow puts one hand on Louisa's shoulder, the other on Solomon's. "I was just asking your brother and sister if the four of you could stay here for good. Would you like that?"

Louisa's face lights up like sunshine sparkling on water. "Can we?" she asks, and then, just as quickly, her shoulders slump. "But would we be bound out?"

The widow shakes her head. "Of course not. You'd be just like my own children."

Solomon stares at the widow, then wiggles away and wraps his arms around my leg, his thumb in his mouth. "I want Mama," he whispers.

I feel myself leaning one way, then the other, like prairie grass in a changing wind. Mama might want us to stay here. She'd say it was better for us to be fed well, and to have some book learning. But Papa would never stand for us to be where they keep slaves. And he told us to go home to Grandma, no matter what.

I glance at Moses. He holds his head high. For the first time, I notice the dark line of hair above his lip. His eyes are steady on mine. Even though it's hard, I know what we have to do.

"Thank you for your kindness, ma'am," I tell the widow, "but we must keep traveling on to our grandmother."

Moses clears his throat. His voice breaks, then deepens, until he almost sounds like Papa. "We promised our father, on his deathbed, that we'd go home to our people," he says.

The Widow Hopkins stands up. She's almost as tall as Moses and her eyes seem icy cold. Louisa shies like a colt and skitters over next to us. I want to bolt, but I force my feet to stay still. I stroke Solomon's curls to calm the shaking inside me.

"You children are stubborn and ungrateful," the widow says. "Moses's foot may never heal, if you keep traveling, and it's dangerous. Think how sick you were when we found you. And what about the little ones? Shouldn't they have a good home?"

Now she's making me mad. My face and neck feel hot. "They *will* have a good home," I tell her, forgetting that we don't even know if Grandma's still alive. "And if you want, we'll give everything back." I bend over to unlace my boots.

Louisa starts to cry. "Can't I keep my new doll?"

The widow puts out her hand. "Don't be so proud, Jesse. You children may keep everything I gave you. It's all useless to me now." She stalks into the house.

"Whew." Moses lets out his breath with a sigh. "We sure made her cross."

"I don't care." I look up into his dark eyes, so much like Papa's. "You could have left us here, and gone west by yourself. Did you think of that?"

He looks a little ashamed. "Only for a minute. We're still a family, Jess." He reaches out his arms, pulling us all into a tight circle. "Even without Mama and Papa."

≈ 20 ≈

A Stranger at the Door

July 15–20, 1828.

East to the Little Sandy River.

The next morning, we're in our wagon again. Louisa and Solomon settle in back with Sandy, whose paws and ears seem even bigger after the widow's good food. The wagon is loaded with jugs of fresh water and enough cornmeal, beans, and pork rind to last us another week.

But the Widow Hopkins won't come out to see us off. Only Emmy is there to say good-bye, tears streaming down her brown cheeks. I can hardly see her, my own eyes are so wet. All four of us wave until the widow's brick house has disappeared beyond the crest of the hill.

"Someday, I'll buy Emmy's freedom," I tell Moses.

I expect him to scoff at me, but instead he nods.

"I'll help you if I can," he says. "I still feel bad we couldn't bring George with us." We lean close together, our shoulders almost touching, for a long time.

Emmy's uncle has given us good directions. We follow the Licking River for a few days down to Blue Lick. The mule's tongue rubs back and forth over the ground, eating up the salt. The mud around the lick is covered with animal tracks: deer, fox, even a bear. That makes us nervous, so we move on, following the buffalo trace up over the first range of hills to Tygart's River.

When the trail is steep, Louisa and I have to walk beside the wagon, but we don't mind. The air is cooler as we climb up onto the ridges, and the tight hills and shadowy hollows remind me we're close to home. Bright red cardinals flit across the trail. Louisa and I pick big bunches of daisies and braid them into wreaths for our hair.

The trail passes by rocky ledges with hollows under them, like open caves. One night, when it rains, we take shelter in a stone room as big as the widow's front parlor. We find ashes from an old fire and build our own in the same spot. Our fire is smoky but it keeps the mosquitoes away. We lean back against the damp walls and watch the rain drip from the edge of the stone shelf above us. "Look, Solomon," Louisa says, lining her dolls up beside her. "Pretend this is our new house."

As we come closer to the Little Sandy, we stop worrying about getting bound out. We tell strangers our grandma is right down the road, and no one bothers us.

One hot afternoon, we come over the top of a ridge. The birds are still, and the leaves of the sycamore trees seem heavy under the sun. Down below, a pale brown river—just the color of our puppy—twists and turns through a narrow valley. Everyone gets down from the wagon, even Moses. We don't say a word.

Finally, Solomon whispers, "Is that it?" When Moses nods, he whoops, "Look, Sandy! There it is! The Little Sandy!" He claps his hands.

Sandy lifts his head and howls like a real coon dog. "He knows this is *his* river," Louisa says, and tugs his ears.

That last hill is steep. It's hard to go down slow, but we do. "No more runaway wagons," Moses says. He and I hold Sadie back until our hands are hot with blisters. We eat a quick, cold supper by the river. "Let's keep traveling," Moses says, even though it's getting dark. We scramble back into the wagon. No one wants to stop now.

Louisa and Solomon fall asleep in back, but Moses and I take turns with the reins, singing to stay awake. The moon lights up the dirt track. Near dawn, we pass the sawmill Papa talked about. Even Sadie seems to know where we are. She trots at a fast clip. When the road forks, she takes the right turning without being told.

"We made it!" I cry, hugging Moses. His face turns red, but he doesn't push me away. I shake Solomon and Louisa. "Wake up!" I tell them. "We're almost home."

They squeeze in beside us on the seat. We pass the big oak tree, and Moses and I speak out loud together, repeating Papa's last instructions: "Not the first turning after the oak, but the second . . ."

Sadie trots so fast, she almost tips the wagon on the turn. We squeal, holding on tight. Sandy jumps out and runs beside us, his nose snuffling the ground.

We pull Sadie up in the clearing. It's not quite light, but smoke already streams from Grandma's chimney. The cabin looks smaller than I remember. We climb down and help Moses onto his crutches. Two geese come flapping from the shed, their necks stretched out flat, hissing and honking. Sandy yelps and skitters under the wagon. Solomon and Louisa cling to my skirts.

The door swings open. "Grandma!" Solomon screams.

But it's not our grandma at all. A tall, skinny woman with a baby on her hip steps out, squinting in the dim light. She shakes her head. "Land sakes," she says. "Homer!" she calls over her shoulder, "look what the cat dragged in!"

21

'Where's My Grandma?'

July 20, 1828.

On the banks of the Little Sandy River.

A man peers over the woman's shoulder, rubbing his eyes, while we stand in a silent row, unsure of what to do. My mouth is dry as dust. Solomon and Louisa clutch my hands. Finally, Solomon blurts out, "Who are *you?* Where's my Grandma?"

The woman shakes her head and runs her eyes over all of us. I'm ashamed of how shabby we look. We haven't had a proper wash since we left the widow's.

"My word," the woman says. "These are Rebecca's children. Who would have thought . . ."

"Don't be rude now, Etta," the man says. "I'm Homer Peters," he tells us. "You come on in."

"It's all right," Moses whispers to us. "Homer is

some kind of cousin to Grandma." We stumble to the cabin. My heart is down around my ankles.

As we gather in the front room, the woman called Etta whispers, "Your Grandma's not in her right mind. About four or five weeks ago, she took to her bed. Hasn't spoke since. She don't eat much, but Doctor says there's nothin' wrong. We were afraid she was fixin' to die—so we come on over to help."

I can't stand it anymore. "We want to see her."

"She's still asleep," Etta says, "and she cain't talk to you—"

I don't care how rude we are. We push on past, hurrying to the closed door beyond the kitchen. I open it carefully. Grandma lies in the middle of her bed, her hands crossed the way Mama's were in her coffin—but Grandma's chest rises and falls under her faded quilt.

I can hardly breathe. The room is stuffy and hot. And Grandma looks so old! Her face is shriveled and sunken, like Louisa's dried apple doll. Her long braid, falling over her shoulder, has turned white. I blink hard, holding back tears. This isn't how I pictured it. I thought Grandma would be waiting in the clearing, her arms open wide—

Louisa breaks the spell. "Grandma," she sobs, and climbs onto the bed, patting Grandma's cheek with her skinny hand. Grandma's eyes flutter open and we cluster around her, nestling on the bed like baby chicks come home to roost. We grab her hands and hold on tight. Everyone is crying, even Moses.

Grandma raises herself to her elbows and sits up so she can pull us all close. Her gray eyes, so like Louisa's, spill over. She traces each one of our faces with her fingers, as if she can't see. "I'm Jesse," I tell her, when her hand flutters over me. "And Moses, Solomon, and Louisa—you remember us, don't you?"

She nods. Then she goes very still, looking over our heads at the empty doorway, her eyes searching.

I swallow hard. "They're both gone, Grandma," I tell her.

She pulls me close. "I felt it inside." Her voice is all croaky, like a frog. "But no one believed me."

"Grandma, you can talk like the rest of us!" Moses says, half laughing, half crying. "You sure fooled your cousins."

Footsteps scritch across the floor and Sandy rushes in, wriggling all over. He jumps up, planting his muddy front paws on Grandma's quilt.

"Sandy, no!" I scold, but Grandma shakes her head.

"Let him be," she says, and strokes his long ears.

"His name is Sandy," Louisa says, "after your river." And then she adds, in a brave voice, "You can keep him, if you want."

Grandma smiles through the tears that trickle down her wrinkled cheeks. " 'Bout time I got me a dog," she says. "Now tell me. What happened?"

"You want to hear all of it?" I ask.

She nods. "Every last bit. From the very beginning—to when you pulled up to my doorstep."

I take a deep breath. "It's a long story," I say.

She pulls us close. "That's just fine. We got all the time in the world."

And so—we begin.

A Note to Readers

I first wrote *Orphan Journey Home* as a serialized story for newspapers. Writing a serial novel was both challenging and exciting. Each chapter was limited to 750 words and had to end with a cliffhanger so the reader would search for the story in the newspaper the following week. Once I got used to the form, I enjoyed the challenge of fitting an adventure story into a tight space.

As the story began to appear in newspapers around the country, I also discovered that I had been given a rare opportunity. Usually, a book is printed and bound before I receive feedback from readers, and then it is too late to make changes. With the serial, I had the chance to include some of my readers' suggestions as I expanded the story for publication as a book.

Newspaper readers have a fine eye for details. They make predictions about what might happen the next week, and are eager to share their thoughts with one another and with the author. Readers of all ages plied me with probing and insightful questions. They wrote me letters, raised their hands at school assemblies, and spoke up at teachers' workshops. Readers had questions about the characters and the journey. They were curious about historical facts. They asked about elements of the story that I had omitted because each chapter had to be short.

I hope that some of you, reading this book, will discover the spots where I responded to your thoughtful ideas. For readers who had questions about historical details, here are some answers to your most frequent questions.

Many children wondered, "Where did you get the idea for *Orphan Journey Home?*"

The novel is based on a true story I uncovered while reading the autobiography of Bethenia Owens-Adair, an early Oregon pioneer. Bethenia's mother, Sarah Damron, was one of six children who were orphaned in 1828 as the family traveled from southern Illinois to eastern Kentucky. The Damron parents died of a disease Bethenia called "milk fever." In spite of their grief, the children made the difficult journey home to their grandmother without much adult help. In the original story, the oldest child was twelve, and the youngest a baby.

Although Bethenia only devoted a few short pages

to her mother's story in her autobiography, I couldn't forget it. I was inspired by the incredible courage, resourcefulness, and family loyalty of these children. When I was asked, a few years later, to write a novel for the newspapers, I decided that the story of the Damron children would lend itself to the serial format.

Learning that the story was based on a true family's experience, many readers asked, "How much of the story is made up?"

Orphan Journey Home—like many of my novels— is based on a mixture of fact and fiction. A number of incidents in the story are based on real events. The Damron children's father really did give them instructions on how to find their way home, when he was on his deathbed. He also provided them with a letter of protection. In their travels, the children actually encountered a man who kept a coffin in his parlor, as well as a wealthy, slave-owning family who offered them a home and an education.

Although I made the family smaller and invented most of the incidents in the story, I tried to include accurate historical details. As far as possible, the Damron family travels on the early trails that I found on historical maps of Illinois and Kentucky. The dangers the Damron family faces are also as true to the time period as I could make them.

"What was milk fever?" many readers wondered. "And why did the parents die—but not the children?"

It took months of detective work to unscramble this puzzle. I talked to doctors, poison specialists, veterinarians, and plant specialists. I read many accounts about diseases of that time. Finally, long after the serial appeared in newspapers, I was reading Russell Freedman's biography of Abraham Lincoln. Freedman described how young Abe's mother died of a disease called "the milksick," or "milk sickness." The illness was caused by a cow eating the poisonous plant called white snakeroot.

Finally, I had some concrete information! I did more research and discovered that there were epidemics of milk sickness in Indiana and Illinois during the time the Damron children were traveling. The more I read, the more I was convinced that this was the disease that killed the Damron parents.

From my mother's veterinary books, I learned that when a cow ate the plant, the poison went into her milk. Her flesh could also become poisonous. A sick animal would shake, lose its appetite, and become weak. Other accounts, written years ago, described human victims becoming very cold. Some said their tongues would turn white, then brown.

Milk sickness can still be a problem for animals today, but rarely for humans. The milk we drink comes from many different cows. When it is all pooled together, any poison is very diluted.

A final puzzle remains: We don't know why some family members died while others escaped the disease. Imagine how different American history would be if Abraham Lincoln had also died of "the milksick!"

Some children asked me, "What is 'fever and ague?' "

We now call this disease malaria. It is still common in many parts of the world. During the time when the Damron children were traveling through Kentucky, people believed that living near streams and rivers was unhealthy, but they thought it was the damp air that caused fever and ague. They didn't realize that mosquitoes—which breed in wet areas—carried malaria, spreading it from one person to the next through their bites. However, some doctors had access to a medicine made from the bark of the cinchona tree in Peru. This bark is a source of quinine—which was the most common medicine used to treat malaria until World War II.

A girl in a Connecticut school was upset by the story's sad beginning. "Why did the parents have to die?" she asked.

Unfortunately, the Damron children lived at a time when many of today's medicines had not yet been invented. There were no shots to protect people against common diseases, and doctors didn't realize that many illnesses are caused by bacteria and viruses, which spread from one person to another when they cough, sneeze, or don't wash their hands.

Even though people didn't understand the cause of disease, women like Jesse's mother often knew which herbs and plants could help when someone was sick. They knew that willow bark, for instance, would help to bring down a fever. (The bark contains aspirin.) They had learned that the foxglove, or digitalis plant, could help heart disease. (Digitalis is still used for heart problems today.) Knowledge about healing herbs and plants was often passed down from a mother to her daughters.

In Dayton, Ohio, a boy asked me, "Can you explain what it means to be 'bound out'?"

In the early years of the nineteenth century, orphaned children had no rights. If they had no relatives to take them in, these children were sometimes "bound out," which was similar to becoming an indentured servant. Adults could keep these orphans until they were eighteen, or even twenty-one. Children could be bound out by their own parents if they were too poor to feed them. Children who were being mistreated by a parent might also be bound out to another family to keep them safe—similar to placing a child in a foster home today.

Some children who were bound out were treated well, while others suffered in their new homes. The adults who kept the children were expected to educate them, although many white owners refused to teach African-American children to read and write. The adults were also supposed to give these children a skill—such as sewing, carpentry, farming, boat building, masonry, or weaving. Some bound-out children received a horse, a Bible, and a new suit or dress at the end of their stay.

The issue of slavery was upsetting to many readers. When I talked with some high school students in Ohio, an African-American boy came up to me at the end of my program. "Why couldn't the Damron children rescue George, and take him with them to Kentucky?" he asked. Then he quickly answered his own question. "Of course—Kentucky was a slave state. I guess it wouldn't be safe to take him there."

"What else could they do?" I asked.

He thought a minute. "At least have the kids think about George again," he said—a suggestion that I promptly added to the story.

In 1828, the year this story takes place, America did not offer equal rights to all its citizens. When the framers of the Declaration of Independence wrote that "all men are created equal," they meant white men who owned property. Women couldn't vote, and had few legal rights. Slaves, most Native Americans, and children—especially orphans—had no rights at all.

At that time, the country was deeply divided by the issue of slavery. In some states, slavery was forbidden. Others—such as Illinois—began as slave states, but then outlawed slavery when they wrote their constitutions. Most southern states, including Kentucky, allowed slavery until the end of the Civil War.

Even though slavery was legal in Kentucky, some residents opposed it. They agreed with the English traveler Morris Birkbeck, who wrote in 1818 that slavery "is the leprosy of the United States, a foul blotch which . . . contaminates the entire system." Other residents of Kentucky relied on slaves to work their plantations; some even made their fortunes raising slaves and selling them as if they were cattle. Many families were split down the middle on the issue of slavery, which led to brothers, sons, fathers, and cousins fighting one another during the Civil War.

A final question, posed by a number of teachers, was: "Why did Jesse's father think the Masons would help his children?"

During the nineteenth century, the Brotherhood of Masons (also known as Freemasons) was one of the few organizations that was dedicated to helping widows and orphaned children. The Masons were a fraternity, or group of men, who had probably begun as European stone cutters sometime in the Middle Ages. Many of America's early leaders, such as Benjamin Franklin and George Washington, were Masons. They believed in education and in religious freedom. They were also dedicated to helping those in need. (In fact, Masons today still follow this mission. They give millions of dollars to charity every year, and their Shriners' Hospitals are open to anyone, free of charge.) For these reasons, William Damron believed his "fellow Masons" would protect his children from harm and help them find their way home.

With all these dangers and threats to their safety, the real-life Damron children were lucky to survive. Sarah Damron (the model for Jesse, in this story) continued to have an adventurous life. When she was sixteen, she married Thomas Owens, who took her back to the western prairies. They farmed in Missouri, but once again, Sarah was living on bottom land that gave the family "fever and ague." A few years later, the Owens family joined a wagon train headed for Oregon. Sarah's second daughter,

Bethenia, became the first woman doctor in the Pacific Northwest. Bethenia inherited the courage, sense of adventure, and pioneer spirit that the Damron children had shown so long ago, when they set out to find their grandmother on the Little Sandy River.

For more information about Liza Ketchum's books for young people, as well as her author programs, please visit her website: www.lizaketchum.com

$15.00

DATE			

JAN   2001